Chronicles of My Alien Invasion Life

By

Jes McCutchen

Manustrium Media
848 S Indianapolis Ave
Tulsa OK 74112

Cover Illustration | Ezra Blank
Cover Design | Max Vittor
Editor | Jeni Chappelle
Interior Formatting | Racheal Daodu

Library of Congress Control Number | 2022906119
ISBN eBook: 979-8-9859486-0-8
ISBN Print Edition: 979-8-9859486-1-5

While a work of fiction, this book is full of anecdotes and shenanigans from my youth, and Chuck and her friends love each other like my friends and I loved each other.

This one is for the Weirdos.

Chapter 1

Our whole lives, Ghost and I were constantly trying to one-up each other on our adventure-having. Determined to find evidence of the paranormal or the otherworldly. Looking for signs that there was something bigger out there for us to discover. If one of us could imagine it, the other would help them see it through. We never had to convince the other to go along with anything. We were just up for whatever it was, no matter how poorly thought through.

So, I didn't question anything when he said, "I found something we have to check out. Bring your swimsuits, everyone."

We tossed our suits and towels into the back of Corrin's fifteen-year-old Honda Accord which, according to her parents, was part of the Oklahoma Teenager Starter Pack. We'd all learned to drive that summer. Only Corrin had a car though, so when it was time to get our licenses, hers was the one we were most excited about.

We'd spent a lot of time exploring the larger state parks around our town and hunting for unexplored caves. We'd done a bit of geocaching too for about two days, but Bailey and Pacey had insisted that using our cell phones wasn't "an authentic woodsy experience."

Ghost's directions took us a few miles north of town, past the dump and the green waste facility. Bailey and Ghost were really into studying maps. They were still doing scouts, and one badge was for how to read topographical maps.

We went over about thirty railroad track crossings and finally came to a dead end near a bridge with a railroad track running over it.

"Nope, nope, nope," Corrin said when she realized we were going to be walking across.

"It's abandoned, I promise," Ghost insisted. "Trains haven't run here in ages."

"Then why can't we just drive the car across?" Pacey looked the track up and down.

"Um, I'm not sure it would hold us?" Ghost hopped out, slinging on his backpack.

"Cool, cool, cool," I said, but of course followed at his heels.

"Fine, but y'all better take it slow," Corrin said, almost at the same time Bailey and Ghost raced each other across.

It was an extremely high bridge, and the creek under it was just a creek. And a creek during a drought.

"We could make a bigger creek with a garden hose," Pacey pointed out as the slightly more cautious three of us made our way across.

"Definitely no diving allowed." I laughed.

"How do you expect us to swim here?" Corrin demanded, hands on her hips.

"I don't," Ghost replied loudly over his shoulder.

The bridge was old. Lots of track had been laid in the last hundred years to bring cattle up into Kansas. A lot of the lines weren't in use anymore. There was a small barrier gate with a chain that had rusted loose a long time ago, so it swung by the hinges. The wood seemed sturdy enough though, and it wasn't like bridges just spontaneously collapsed.

Right?

Except that one time with Mothman. But I was pretty sure Mothman was trying to warn everyone anyway, and if he showed up, I was on the lookout.

"What are those?" Pacey pointed at some markings that looked almost like carvings in the metal parts of the bridge.

"I'm not sure," I said. "Graffiti?"

"Well, yes, obviously graffiti, but what does it say?"

"I'm not even sure what language it is," I gave their shoulder a nudge. "Probably aliens."

Pacey laughed, "You wish."

We were both still looking up at the markings when Corrin caught up with us.

"Those are weird," she said.

"Yeah, I think so too." I pulled out my phone and snapped a picture to look at later, and we went to catch up with the boys.

We made it across without incident and walked about a quarter of a mile. Then we came to a gravel road that ran parallel to part of the track.

"I think they used this for maintenance, but it's a back way to the quarry," Ghost said, excited to have found the road he had hoped to. "Not much further."

"Good, because I'm hot," I whined.

"Yeah you are," Corrin said in a singsong voice, and I felt a bit faint.

"Here ya go, steamy." Pacey passed me a water bottle.

Ghost was right though, and our destination wasn't too much further.

"What is this?" Bailey asked.

All five of us stared out at the otherworldly landscape for the first time.

The road leading down carved into the cliffside, unlike any naturally formed one. The edges were severe, steep, and cleanly cut. Layers and layers of earth in rainbow striations. The deep familiar reds of Oklahoma outshined all the tans and grays and yellows and blues. The ochre and the mauve. When the sun shined brightly, the layers sparkled like glitter.

When the Quarriors—I assumed that was what you called someone who worked at a quarry—were done, they filled it with run off overflow from a nearby lake, diverted to help it keep from flooding in stormy seasons. But eventually the engineers had come up with new ways to handle the overflow, so they'd left the quarry on its own.

"How deep is it?" Pacey asked.

"The map says hundreds of feet," said Ghost.

The water was still as glass. It reflected the sun and blue sky, and for a minute, everything felt silent as we took it in.

"How do we get down?" Corrin asked.

"We jump," Ghost said with his most lopsided and impish grin.

I grinned back at him.

Corrin rolled her eyes. "And how do we get back up?"

"We climb?" Ghost said.

"Dang it, Ghost, you don't know, do you?" Bailey asked, laughing.

"Let's go ahead and figure that out so we don't all drown in a giant box full of water, shall we?" I said, and we started walking.

Eventually, we saw some birds land, and it broke the magic of the water's surface for a moment, but otherwise, everything was serene and stayed enchanting while we searched along the edge for a path down.

It didn't take too long before we found one. It was narrow and carved out of the rocks. There were the remnants of a wooden platform near the top, that we guessed could have been an area for site managers to look out from. It zigzagged down almost to the water, but with a few handholds, we were able to get out.

"Is the water safe?" I asked.

"I actually brought something to test that," Bailey said excitedly and pulled out a water analysis kit, because of course he had one of those.

"You just had those on you?" Pacey examined the kit.

Bailey shrugged. "Always be prepared."

"I'm really gonna have to get into that water, aren't I?" Corrin asked.

"Only if you want to," I said. She knew that, but it always felt good to remind each other. These humans were the only ones I felt myself around, and yeah, there was peer pressure, but we prided ourselves in it being the good kind.

She smiled at me, and I melted a bit like I did every time she smiled at me.

"We'll see," she said, "and tomorrow is wash day anyway."

"We're all clear," Bailey smiled at a strip of litmus paper that was bright blue.

"You sure it's supposed to be blue?" Pacey teased.

"I mean, don't like swallow a ton, but we're not going to disintegrate."

"Always so reassuring, Bailey." I chuckled as I pulled on goggles.

Ghost and I hopped into the water, and immediately, it was impossible to feel the bottom. Unlike a lake or a river or the ocean, the quarry just dropped off in a sheer slice.

I did a few breast strokes out away from the edge and dove under. The water was cool but not cold. The heat from the sun had warmed the rocks, and the water, though stagnant, was massive.

Gauging where we would jump from, I dove under and swam around, looking for rocks or rusty cars or oil drums. But there was nothing but clear water down further than the sunlight reached. I'd never been in water so deep, and it was disorienting until I broke back through the surface.

"Find any treasures?" Bailey asked from the path.

"No, nothing." I gave them all a thumbs up. I dove in again and swam in a big circle, coming up for air when I needed to, making sure it was clear.

"Yep, we're all clear," Ghost said.

"I'm staying here to drag your asses out if you need me to." Corrin pointed finger guns at us. She was actually the strongest swimmer out of all of us. Her parents put her and her brothers in swim lessons when they were really young, and she'd done lifeguard training two summers ago. Even though she said the thought of actually working as a lifeguard bored her to tears.

"Spending all day yelling at kids for running by the pool and forgetting to take their goggles off on the high dive?" she'd said. "No, thank you."

The four of us made it up to the top, where the small platform was, and peered over the edge.

"Who's going first?" Ghost asked with his grin wide.

The rest of that day was a blur.

If I'd had to guess, I'd have said we'd all jumped off that cliff two dozen times a piece. Each time felt like flying. Like falling into a new part of the world. Breaking the surface feet first, then feeling bolder, diving, doing flips.

Watching from above was as much fun as watching from below. We cheered each other on as we sailed through the air. Eventually, even Corrin took some turns, wrapping her hair tightly in a swim cap. Pacey got comfortable enough to swim shirtless but kept their binder on. We shared snacks and looked for fish. And the whole day flew by in a whirlwind of splashes and *Jaws* references.

We walked back to the car a little before sunset, tired and slightly sunburned. As we crossed the bridge, almost back at the main road, Pacey stopped again to look at the symbols.

"Do those look different to you?" they asked, and I peered up at them in the setting light.

"Maybe?"

"Weird," they said.

"Come on, you all, I don't want to be late, this ride is leaving," Corrin called from the other side.

We went home laughing and leaning against one another in the crowded compact sedan, arms full of wet towels and backpacks and reusable water bottles. Bailey passed around Polaroid pictures he'd taken of each of us, and I held onto mine, tucking it into my bedroom mirror when I got home.

Chapter 2

When Ghost finally told me his idea that maybe what we were seeing at the quarry was something more than a mirage, it didn't come as a surprise.

"I think it's a portal, Chuck," he said while we sat in the sun, eating Sno Cones. His long tan legs stretched out in front of him as he gazed into the distance.

"A portal to where?" I crunched the sugary ice between my teeth.

"I'm not sure, but I have some theories." He didn't elaborate. "I think we'll really be able to see it at night." When he asked for my help convincing everyone to come out to the quarry at night a few days later, instead of during the hot afternoon sun, I didn't hesitate.

And, as usual, when Ghost and I had convinced each other something was a good idea, the two of us could convince our friends to come along as well.

"Just tell your folks you're spending the night at my house." I was working on Corrin and hoping she would drive us to the cliffs before nightfall and after whatever experiment Ghost had in mind had worked its way out of his system.

"I just think it's an absurdly stupid idea to quarry jump at night," she said for the third time.

"But we know our way around so well." I rolled over onto my stomach, giving her a pouty face.

"And we'll have our caving headlamps with us," Ghost added. "They're waterproof."

"Wearing goggles on your face when you jump into the deep end is the first rookie mistake of the high dive, dummies," Corrin said.

"Obviously, the people at the bottom will have the lights. You know, to show us where to land and swim to and stuff. It'll be fun, I promise," I said. "I also have these."

Then, I pulled my trump card.

I dramatically unzipped my backpack to show all the makings for about fifty s'mores.

As though drawn by the sweet scent of marshmallow, Bailey looked up from his notebook and said, "I'm in."

"You should have led with the s'more part," Pacey said, practically drooling. They reached for the bag.

"Not yet, you cretin," I said, swatting their hand away. "Back, you fiend."

"Okay," Corrin finally agreed. "But we're bringing my telescope."

There was a simultaneous groan from the other three because the telescope was huge and, while, yes, the end result always had us mouths agape and in awe of the universe, it meant three people in the back had to ride with the massive instrument across their legs because it was "too precious to cram into the trunk."

Corrin smirked and crossed her arms. "Either the telescope goes, or y'all are walking."

"Shotgun!" all four of us yelled at once.

"I have the s'mores," I added, thus securing my place up front.

9

"That means we should probably leave soon so we can get everything calibrated before it's too dark," Ghost said.

"Time to tell some fibs, folks," I said, and we all texted or called our various guardians. It was only for one night, and they'd let us go camping before, just not on such short notice and definitely not at the quarry.

Then, piling into Corrin's car, we headed just out of town, down the same road we'd driven a thousand times before.

The five of us got to the turnoff before sunset and together hauled the telescope and our camping gear. It took two trips to get everything, and on the way, Ghost and I stopped to study the markings Pacey had pointed out to me on the bridge.

The symbols still meant nothing to me, but Ghost was writing them down so quickly, I felt like he must have been studying them pretty closely.

The night was clear and crisp and a cool relief from the constant pounding heat of the summer. Oklahoma really loved to get its swelter on.

Corrin got to work setting up the telescope, and Bailey helped her get the Orion software up and running so we could more easily track the planets and any comet she might have targeted as worth checking out.

We rarely got far enough out of town to use the telescope, and each summer, the city lights got a bit more sprawling. Luckily, we didn't have to pull the telescope on our bikes in a makeshift wagon trailer anymore so we could cover further distances. All hail driver's ed.

The stars were out in the trillions, and we gathered armloads of firewood so we could have it ready when we were done looking through the telescope. It was warm enough we technically didn't need a fire, but no camp-out would have been complete without one. And how else would we get the beans heated and the marshmallows roasted?

"We're going to jump." I pulled off my jeans and kicked off my tennis shoes. I had come prepared with a swimsuit on, and I handed Pacey the underwater lights.

"Sure you don't want to go look around at the bottom first?" they said, laughing. "The giant octopus might be prowling."

I wished that hadn't made me hesitate. But in Oklahoma, we took our cryptids seriously, and the giant lake octopus was known to collapse whole boats.

"Wait, this isn't a lake," I said.

Pacey laughed, clearly seeing the train of thought cross my face. "I wondered where you went there for a second," they said. "Meet you at the bottom."

Ghost was staring out at the starlight reflecting off the perfectly still water.

"It should be easier to see any minute now," he said in a whisper.

"And you want us to just like, jump onto it?" I asked equally quietly. I was not totally sure what was about to happen, but it felt magnitudinous.

"I'm thinking it'll be more like jumping *into* it?" he said with a question in his voice. "But I'm not sure. I just know it seems consistent."

I nodded. It made sense. At least if the whole portal theory was accurate.

"And whatever happens, I'm glad we're doing this together." He smiled at me.

I peered up at him. "You really expect something big to happen, don't you?"

"We'll just have to see."

We waited for what felt like ages but was probably only a few minutes. Then it happened.

It shimmered in the air.

We could see the supposed portal clearly now. Much more so than during the daylight. It was lit up like a dim neon sign.

My instinct was to call out to the others, to see if they could see it too.

But Ghost just said, "Let's go!" and took off toward the edge.

I jumped just seconds behind Ghost. He had slightly longer legs and a stronger push and went a little further than I did.

Like we had done a trillion times before but with a different amount of purpose.

When Ghost and I jumped that night, the air felt... different. Neither of us knew what exactly we were jumping into, though I suspected Ghost knew much more than he let on.

But we were both excited to see where we landed.

You know what it's like when you think there's one more step on a staircase, but there's not? Or when it's super late at night and you sit down on the toilet in the bathroom before you realize the lid is shut?

Or when you're a little kid and your grandma cleaned the sliding glass door so well for company at Thanksgiving that you walked right into it? And Thanksgiving was totally ruined because your nose was broken and you walked through doors a little more slowly after that.

It was like that, but also, it felt like a full minute of landing.

It was slow motion.

Ghost fell through it, like seeing someone at the top of a tube slide at the park. He just sort of got swallowed up.

Then whatever it was—a wormhole? A portal?

It closed.

And for a split second, it was solid. I hit it. My legs crushed on themselves. A crack.

Then it was gone.

I was in the water, and there was a sharp yell.

Then, I was under the water, and everything was quiet.

When I woke up, I was spitting up a half gallon of quarry water and coughing so hard it felt like my chest was ripping open. Later on, we'd figure out that it was actually Bailey giving me CPR that caused my broken ribs.

And there was so much yelling.

I wanted to sit up, but I couldn't move.

"Keep looking. I've got Chuck." Bailey moved to hold my neck, and I realized Corrin had been bracing my head.

I tried to look out at the water. From the corner of my eye, I could see Pacey swimming in circles. The light from their headlamp bobbed as they dove into the water over and over and over.

Corrin dove in and did the same.

Each time they surfaced, they screamed his name.

"Help is on the way, Chuck," Bailey said. "You have to hold still though. Don't move, okay?"

"What happened?" I asked. My throat was raw, and I was having trouble focusing on anything.

"You fell and got hurt," he said. "We're looking for Ghost."

"I think he went through," I said.

Then I must have blacked out. The next thing I remembered was being in an ambulance, and Corrin was there holding my hand. They must have given me some pretty good pain meds because I couldn't feel much at that point.

The next few days were a blur, and I was mostly out of consciousness.

When I woke up for good, I was in a hospital room, and Pacey was there. They were writing in one of their notebooks, focusing hard on something. I tried to sit up, maybe out of instinct, but my neck was in a brace, and neither of my legs could move.

My arms were free though, and I waved at them until I got their attention.

"You're awake!" Pacey said.

Then to my confusion, they burst into tears. Like, *big* tears. The large, rolling ones that fashionable actresses like Julia Roberts were always able to muster up at the end of Richard Gere movies.

"Hey, hey, yeah, I'm okay." I reached out to pat them on the arm.

They laughed. "You're ridiculous, Chuck. Don't comfort me."

"Fine, I won't. But I need water. Please."

"Oh, of course!" They grabbed a tiny paper cup with a straw from the tray next to my hospital bed. They held it out to me, and I took two long refreshing gulps, till they yanked it away. "No, no, slow down. Grand Chancellor Nurse insists you only take a sip."

"Hey, I'm in pain here." I winced. "Give me the water."

"No way, dude. Just wait till you meet her, I'm not giving you any more," they said. "I have to call your folks, Chuck, but I'll be right back, okay?"

I nodded and closed my eyes. They stepped out into the hallway, and I could hear them telling my folks I was awake and that, yes, they would wait until they showed up.

Pacey came back smiling but still had tears that they hastily wiped away.

"Why the long face?" I asked.

"Your folks wanted me to wait to talk to you. We have some bad news."

"Come on, don't make me wait." I wasn't sure what the news was, but my guess is it had to do with Ghost, so I went with that. "It's Ghost, isn't it?"

Pacey nodded, eyes welling up again. "He's gone, Chuck."

"Well, yeah." I rolled my eyes.

"You knew that?" they asked. "Have you been faking your medically induced coma?"

"No, but I figured he was gone and the portal thingy worked."

"Okay, so you're on the *good* good meds."

"Look, I'll explain it to you more later. But it's fine."

"No, Chuck. Ghost is dead. He never came back up from the water."

I shook my head. "He's not in the water. He's in … maybe a pocket universe? We weren't really clear on that. I probably should have asked him for more details, now that I think about it."

The rest of my conversations with my family and physicians went the same way.

I even got an "I believe that's what you believe" from Corrin, which was basically the most awful thing to hear from anyone but especially from someone you trusted almost all the secrets in your life to.

A little over a month later, the doctors decided my back was as healed as it was going to get in the hospital and I would do better in a physical therapy rehab facility.

The number of times I reminded people what a strong swimmer Ghost was got to feel unreal. But no one would accept that he had just *poof* disappeared into thin air, even though there was obviously a big difference between a portal and thin air.

My counselor in rehab made me try to remember that what had happened to Corrin, Bailey, and Pacey was traumatic too. And they were trying their best to be good friends to me, but the loss of Ghost was a lot for everyone.

But it was hard, feeling like no one was on my side. And I knew I'd probably never find Ghost if I couldn't convince them to help.

Chapter 3

One thing I really wasn't worried about, high school-wise, was being embarrassed. I'll spare you a lot of the details about what happened that summer, but just know I stopped feeling squeamish about the major things after a couple of weeks in intensive hospital care and all the subsequent physical therapy that came with it.

When I say they let it all hang out, I mean all of it.

There is very little that is private when you're in traction and casts and braces and need nurses to help you with everything and all that fun stuff.

I'll skip ahead to when Pacey and Corrin came to visit me, rather than dwell on the tedious in between. I kinda wish the messy stuff wasn't so important or memorable, so I usually just pretend it's a haze and move onto the rehab stuff.

"Thanks for visiting me," I was sitting with Pacey and Corrin outside at the rehab facility, getting a much-needed break from PT and all other types of therapies.

I was in with a lot of little kids too because I jumped right before my birthday, so was technically still a minor.

"Do you mind all the kids around here?" Pacey asked.

"No, but it really makes me miss Arty," I said. My little brother had come up a couple times, but it wasn't the same as having him all up in my space every second.

Around us, there were kids from ages five to around thirteen mostly. Some were recovering from serious injuries or illnesses and just enjoying the sunlight and fresh air. Others were running around with a variety of mobility aids to help them navigate the playground.

It felt a lot like I imagined Camp Half-Blood, and all the staff did a fantastic job of inventing creative ways for us to get into exercise without it feeling boring. I imagined PT for grownups was significantly duller.

"By far, the worst part is the lack of caffeine. So, thank you for this." I held the warm drink in both hands and savored the smell. They'd brought me a massive latte and pastries from our favorite coffee shop, and I probably looked like I was starving when I snatched them both away. "I owe you both a life debt."

"Can I have a sip?" Pacey asked, and I glared at them until they held up their hands, chuckling. "Okay, okay, never mind."

Thank goodness most of the nurse techs would bring me a cup of coffee from their lounge when I asked, but the cafeteria was all juice and milks: whole, almond, soy, oat. They were all about bone density and calcium here.

"I'm on enough meds that the caffeine headache doesn't stand a chance though." I hoped I sounded reassuring.

"Always looking on the bright side," Corrin said. Right as I was about to chug some of the latte, she put her hand over the lid. "That's definitely going to burn you, Chuck. Slow down."

I laughed. "How did I ever survive without you?"

They both shared a glance.

"Sorry. Too soon?" I said.

"I mean, that wasn't really a joke, so no?" Pacey reached over and held my other hand.

"What's going on?" I asked.

Corrin looked down, tears brimming her eyes. I wanted to reach over and wipe them away but chickened out and just handed her a tissue from my pocket.

She looked at it and grimaced, "Ew, Charlene."

"Don't full name me! And what? It's clean, I promise. I'm a granny now. I will always have clean tissues and hard candies along with my cane. Get used to it."

"They stopped the search for Ghost's body," Pacey said somberly.

They both were watching me intently to see how I would react.

"Is that all?" I asked. "There would never have been a body." I shrugged and shoveled some more of the cheese danish into my mouth. "I'm not sure where he is, but his body definitely isn't in that quarry."

"Chuck, we have to talk to you about that." Corrin said.

"About what?" I asked, and Pacey squeezed my hand. "Oh, about how everyone thinks I'm crazy and there aren't actually aliens and Ghost didn't go through a portal of some sort?"

They both nodded and looked at me like a really depressing puzzle.

"Look," I said, leaning forward, "you both know me, better than pretty much anyone except maybe Ghost. I saw it happen. Before I jumped. And besides, how else do you explain all of this?" I gestured to my relatively broken body. "We jumped off that quarry a trillion times and…"

Pacey cut me off. "Oh, no. You misunderstand. I believe you."

"Wait, what?"

"Yeah, and I'm definitely skeptical," Corrin said. "But Pacey and I have been talking, and a lot of what you're saying makes sense. I still think you're bonkers but like in the normal Chuck way."

"You both believe me?"

Corrin clarified, "I said I am skeptical. But that doesn't mean I won't support you."

"So then, what is with the big talk right now?"

"It's our parents," Pacey said. "They want us to spy on you and figure out what's made you go all dead set on aliens being real. We think you might be headed for some more intense mental health rehab. Which, don't get me wrong, you could probably use like in general, but not for this."

"Thanks?" I said.

"No shade. You know I'm all about the anti-anxiety meds and finding a therapist that works for you. But I also know you're telling the truth and that adding a bunch of false diagnoses would be bad for everyone."

"So, what should I do?" I asked them. "I can't exactly say, 'lol JK I was messing with you.' That makes me seem like I'm for sure lying, and you know I'm a terrible liar."

"We're not sure," said Corrin, "But we want to make sure you don't end up like Buffy in that one episode of *Buffy*."

I nodded. I honestly hadn't really given it much thought. Everyone was constantly asking me if I was doing okay, and I'd assumed they meant physically. I could definitely see how the whole alien portal business might raise a few mental wellbeing red flags though. "I'll tone it down, I guess. At least to start."

"And maybe don't bring it up as loudly as you have been around the kids."

"Did you hear about the arts and crafts basket weaving incident?" I grimaced.

"What? No. What did you do?" Pacey asked.

"Do we want to know?" Corrin said, groaning.

"Probably not, but I can show you the art I made later. You can have some."

"Cool. Thanks?" Pacey laughed.

I really hoped I'd get to leave soon.

"We have something for you." From under the picnic table, Corrin pulled out a long package and handed it over. It was wrapped impeccably, in gold-and-silver paper. There was lace ribbon tied in a bow with sprigs of some wildflowers. Her wrapping game was always on point.

It was obviously cane shaped.

"You're giving me your Nintendo Switch?" I squealed. "Corrin, you shouldn't have."

Most of my rehab was going well, but I was having to work really hard to get used to my mobility aid. The PTs assured me I would get used to it and were really encouraging when I told them about weightlifting and LARPing.

They warned me I would need to watch my balance for the rest of my life and probably shouldn't let anyone whack me too hard with a melee weapon but that I'd be moving around again before I knew it.

I got to unwrapping. And revealed what had to be the raddest cane on the planet.

"Did..." I started, and my jaw dropped. "Did you find me a cane that is *cool?*"

Sure enough, I pulled it out the rest of the way and it was a clear amber color. Sleek and opaque, curved like a classic cane and with a no-slip cap on the end so I knew my PT wouldn't make a fuss.

"If you need to return it—" Corrin started to say.

But I cut her off. "It's perfect, thank you."

"You're welcome," she said, smiling warmly.

Just then, the tech walked up to our table, "Hey kiddo, time to tell your friends bye."

"Bye, kiddo." Corrin smiled and gathered up the trash from the table. "We'll see you really soon." She bent down and gave me a quick hug.

"We'll be back next weekend if you're not outta here yet." Pacey ruffled my hair. "Love you, Chuck."

"Back at ya."

Recovery took longer than I wanted it to, but eventually I got released in time to enjoy the last couple weeks of summer, which was a blessed relief. I was so worried they'd keep me stuck at the hospital until school started. I need my summer days and movie nights.

The doctors all agreed I'd need a mobility aid for the rest of time, but I was definitely okay with that, since the alternatives were all awful. Plus, we're all just temporarily able-bodied, and I long ago stopped being self-conscious about needing help for my ADHD-rattled brain.

Having friends like mine didn't hurt either. They were the *literal* best.

The day I got back home, Corrin, Pacey, and Bailey had all come over to my house and decorated my bedroom as a welcome home treat.

They'd stocked my bedside table with a dozens of my favorite snacks—primarily any type of sour candy and a few apples, which I guessed were from Corrin—and gotten me a new, really fancy water bottle they all signed with a note saying it was because they weren't allowed to sign my casts since people don't use those plaster ones anymore. And again, I guessed the water bottle idea was Corrin's because she was all about hydration.

There were also tons of balloons.

Like four hundred balloons.

My mom groaned audibly, and I squealed in delight when we opened up my door and the balloons came pouring into the hallway. They must have filled it in and left through the window.

"Can I help you pop them?" my little brother, Arty, screamed and dove headfirst into the packed room.

"Of course you can," I said, hitting some out of the way with my cane and making my way into the fray. It took a good ten minutes to get enough popped that I could see my bed and all the other gifts they'd left behind.

"They said there would be a few small things," my mom said, shaking her head and chuckling.

By the time we'd gotten the room cleared out enough, I was wiped out. My mom was right to not let me party too hard on my first day back. But being in my own bed for the first time in weeks felt amazing. And it only took a few minutes for me to drift off. I didn't even need to use a sleep app.

When I woke up the next morning, it was to the sound of laughter and dishes clanking in the kitchen. Arty was reading a comic book at the foot of my bed, and I nudged him.

"Who all is here?" I asked.

"Pretty much everyone," he said, grinning.

"All right, then skedaddle so I can make myself presentable."

I made my way downstairs, slowly, stopping by the bathroom to brush my teeth along the way.

In the kitchen, crowded around the table and a giant pile of pancakes, were Pacey, Bailey, and my parents. Corrin and Arty were hard at work, adding more pancakes to an already huge pile.

"Yay!" Pacey hopped up to hug me, followed right away by Bailey and Corrin.

Then my brother piled in as well, and it was almost hard to breathe.

"It's really good to have you back home," Pacey said and sat back down to keep working on their stack of pancakes.

"It's good to be back." I sat down in the open space on the bench seat.

"So, what are your plans for the day?" my parent asked.

I knew what I wanted to do, which was talk to Pacey about anything they may have found out about Ghost's disappearance, but I knew I needed to ease into things. My folks really wanted me to make sure I was ready for school, so I needed to chill a bit.

"Not sure, probably just hang out here?" I accepted the pile of pancakes my brother handed me.

"I need to go by the library," Pacey said. "Maybe it would be okay for you to come along?"

"Is that okay with you two?" I asked, turning toward my folks.

My mom smiled, clearly tired. "Whatever you're comfortable with, sweetie. Just don't wear yourself out. Call us if you need a ride, okay?"

"Okay, great," I said and shoveled a huge fork full of pancake in my mouth.

"Whoa, slow down. You're gonna choke." Bailey said.

"Yeah, and the library is an American institution. It's not going anywhere before we finish our breakfast," Pacey added.

"And we're making more pancakes," my brother exclaimed, waving the spatula around like a wizard.

I was really glad to be home.

Turned out going to the library did, in fact, wear me out, so we left pretty soon after we got there. But it was so great to just be out and about with my friends. Doing nerdy research stuff like checking out books.

Most of my first weeks back consisted of trying to convince myself to do exercises, being scolded by my parents for not doing enough exercises, watching movies in the pool, and putting off my summer reading.

I had to get used to the changes in my mobility as well, but luckily everyone was patient and also not being awkward and trying to avoid the topic. I loved that about my friends. They were nothing if not honest and supportive, and I'm getting emotional just thinking about them right now.

I was able to get back to my other regular activities, like helping with the community fridge and spending a lot of money on Sno Cones.

In the back of my head, though, was the persistent need to find Ghost and make headway on how to do that. I spent a lot of time doing internet searches and finding rabbit holes of information about aliens and UFOs.

But it was really easy for regular stuff, like social media and redecorating my room, to impede big quests, so for a few weeks, not much progress was made.

Chapter 4

"I can't believe this." Corrin collapsed on my bed and draped her long neck over the edge, brown arm thrown across her eyes, like some sort of fainting Victorian lady.

"It's going to be okay," I said, shaking my head. I pulled my frizzy hair up into a messy brown knot and looked into my mirror, trying to decide if I wanted to bother with any makeup before we headed to the high school to pick up our class schedules.

"It will not be okay, Chuck. None of this is okay." She groaned and rolled herself up in my Star Wars comforter like a burrito. "How are we supposed to survive senior year without you *and* Ghost?" She pouted her full lips at Pacey, who was sitting cross-legged on the floor, head bent over their computer.

"I'm not going to be far." Pacey rolled their eyes. "It's an online concurrent enrollment program," they said for the hundredth time. "I'll literally be available any time you need me."

Pacey was smart. Like, super smart. And they had opted to do online learning because, frankly, regular school wasn't going to be engaging enough. Plus it gave them extra time to help me look into alien related things.

"It's still stupid," Corrin said with a huff.

"I wish I was going to be with y'all too, but this is better anyway. I can get more research done." After that, Pacey turned back to their computer tasks, and Corrin, sighing even more loudly, unwrapped herself from the comforter.

Easier said than done, though, and she landed on my floor.

"Get up," I said, pulling her to a seat. "You're a mess. We gotta keep it at least a little bit together."

She shook her head, braids swinging around her shoulders. "Nah, I'm going full dumpster fire. That's the only way this is gonna work."

I laughed and gave her hand a small squeeze.

"Dumpster fire" was pretty much the best way to sum up the past few months. So, I couldn't blame her.

I'd given up trying to even talk to my folks about Ghost. And Pacey had gone full emo-rebel, grownups-don't-know-shit mode. We'd all been coping in different ways, but nothing was filling the hole Ghost left.

Senior year was already going to be hard because of typical high school drama. I might have felt cool around my friends but only because we all spoke fluent nerd.

Now, Corrin, Bailey and I had to face all the rumors about this summer without two of our party and...

"Where is Bailey, by the way?" I asked.

"He should be here by now." Corrin looked down at her phone. The case was one of five matching ones Ghost had custom made for us with all our favorite D&D characters on them.

"I swear he never used to be this late to stuff," Pacey said, and they were right.

"I'll check Steam," I said and flipped to the app on my phone. Sure enough, Bailey was logged in and active. I shot him a DM, reminding him it was back-to-school night for schedule pick up.

He let me know he had indeed forgotten and that he was on the way as soon as he logged off.

"He'll be here in about three minutes." I decided I didn't want to bother with makeup and clicked my Kaboodle shut.

We all more or less grew up together. I'd been backdoor neighbors with Bailey since his family had moved into the neighborhood at the start of second grade. He had complimented my vintage Jurassic Park dino damage toy collection; I complimented his vintage X-Men t-shirt, and the rest was history.

Well, more like a long timeline full of role playing, board games, LARPing, and camping out.

We added Corrin, Pacey, and Ghost to our party over the next couple of years. The five of us as a group really solidified over the need for general survival of the hellscape that was middle school. You couldn't pay me a million dollars to go back through those years, but having each other had made it bearable.

When Bailey got there, he came in through the window as usual. He and I used to climb over the fence until our parents decided it was too dangerous after I cut my leg and needed a couple stitches, and they didn't want us messing up the chain-link any more than we already had. So, they let us put a gate between our houses.

"Hello ladies and gentle-thems," he said by way of greeting and tossed his backpack in, pulling himself after it.

"Hey," we all said in relative unison.

"So, are we agreed that we're starting a new campaign after we wrap up the current one?" he asked hopefully, pulling out character draft sheets and handing them out.

Pacey barely glanced up from whatever they were typing and just added the printout to a stack of papers already piled next to them. Corrin took one look at her sheet and swapped it with mine.

I looked down and smiled. Bailey had been trying to get Corrin to play a mage or other primarily magic role since we started role playing together years ago. Trying to slip one in as a detective mystic would not work on her, and he knew that. Pacey and I were more fluid in our choices of class and trusted Bailey to make the major calls.

Corrin's favorite thing to remind us was that she "was created to bust un-righteous skulls. Tank or nothing for this Xena Warrior Princess."

Today, she just said, "Keep your spell books, Bailey. I'm the muscle."

"Fine, you can be the butcher, but you have to at least wear a talisman," Bailey said. Then after a moment of quiet, he cleared his throat. "Also," he said, and we all looked at him. "I think I found us a fifth player."

The reactions across the board were... less than positive.

"Nope."

"What? No!"

"No way. Ghost is still out there."

I threw a look at Pacey, who spoke last.

"Do you really think that?" Bailey asked.

Everyone was silent, and the only sound in the room was the tinny Dependence Mode song playing from Corrin's phone.

"Yes," they said confidently.

And I loved Pacey as much as I ever had in that moment. They were always there to back me up, and they usually came with facts.

"Y'all have to stop this," Bailey said.

"Why?" I asked. I was frustrated. "We barely ever talk about Ghost anymore. I'd rather talk to Pacey about their theories than just ignore he ever existed."

"No one is ignoring that he existed." Bailey's eyes flashed with hurt. "But we don't have to make up conspiracies about it."

"I'm not making stuff up," Pacey said, giving Bailey a soft look that was also steady. "You know I'm not manipulative or gullible."

"That's not what I meant, and you know it, Pacey," he said.

"Stop fighting, please," said Corrin.

"This isn't a fight," Pacey and Bailey said at the same time.

I laughed, tucking my thumbs into the holes in my hoodie sleeves and grabbing my cane. "Look," I said, "I want to know what happened, and we can't do that by ignoring what I saw. Pacey, I want to know what you're thinking. Bailey, I want to also be a rational, reasonable, and smart person. And I don't want to add a fifth party member. Because I'm sad, and I'm tired, and the three of you are the only people on the planet I can be myself around." My voice cracked, and I glanced at the clock. "Oh shit, and we're going to be late."

"Fine, let's go, but I really think having someone else to play with isn't a bad idea," Bailey said as we gathered up our things. "Even if Ghost comes back, we could still play with six."

"She knows that, buddy." Corrin patted him on the shoulder.

"I'm standing right here," I said.

"And she's standing right here," Corrin said.

"Don't mock me."

"And I'm mocking her."

I grabbed my phone, and we all headed out the door.

"This is my worst freaking nightmare," I whispered and reached for Bailey's arm with my free hand. My other hand held my cane, and I worried I might literally collapse like an overheated Bronte character, but there was no Star Wars comforter to soften the landing so I remained upright.

"What in the fresh, food court, trash can is this?" Corrin asked, her mouth agape.

Outside the school, what looked like half the senior class was standing around a gigantic poster of Ghost. His full name, Samuel Anderson, was scrawled across it in honest-to-goodness bubble letters. None of his friends had called him anything but Ghost since seventh grade.

"Are they singing a praise and worship song?" Bailey's voice thick with disbelief.

"Yes, Bailey, I believe they are," Corrin said, her eyes wide.

"And are they holding their cell phones up like candles?" I blinked rapidly. This had to be a nightmare. Should I rub my eyes? I settled for pinching Bailey.

"Ow! Hey!" he said.

"Just making sure I'm not dreaming."

"You're supposed to pinch *yourself*, Chuck, not someone else."

"Oh my Hecate, that's Julie Malkie up there," Corrin whispered at me. "Am I really seeing a memorial service for Ghost?"

"Yes, I think we are."

"A cheerleader-led memorial service for Ghost?"

I nodded.

"At school?"

I nodded again and said sarcastically, "I mean, he just loved all our sports teams so much."

"Yeah, you know, now that I think about it, this is pretty much exactly how I would have planned it," Corrin said, nodding and matching my sarcasm.

"Look." I gestured at the crowd, "All his favorite people."

Corrin giggled first. Then Bailey joined in. We got a glare from a few of the students toward the back and from Julie Malkie, and I couldn't help myself. I flipped her off. With both hands. Don't tell my grandma.

"Miss Lapin, off to a great start of senior year, I see."

I swung around, about to justify my momentary loss of decorum, when I saw it was Mr. Jacobs, probably the only teacher Ghost actually liked.

"Oh, sorry, Mr. Jacobs," I said.

"No need to apologize. This is rather contrite," he said, nodding to the group. "But they needed a faculty sponsor, and I thought it might help some students process their emotions."

Corrin was still glaring daggers at Julie, and Bailey was looking down at his feet. Some high schoolers had a way of making things that had nothing to do with them all about them, and this took the cake.

"I suppose none of you even knew about it?" Mr. Jacobs asked.

I shook my head.

He sighed. "People suck."

I let out a barking laugh. "You have no idea."

"Oh, my dear, I teach high school. I know." Then he added softly, "Ghost was a good one. I'm very sorry he isn't here with you all right now."

I noticed he didn't say dead, and I appreciated that, even if he probably meant nothing by the omission. I know there were rumors about me and Ghost and the disappearance and everything, so he may not have said it purposefully, but I liked it anyway.

Now my lip quivered. "Thank you, sir."

"You three might want to go collect your schedules from around the other side of the gym. I'm halfway expecting an altar call, and I wouldn't want you getting into an actual fight before the year even gets going."

"Thanks, Mr. J.," said Corrin, and the three of us took off to grab our schedules.

We picked them up and decided to walk through each one to get a jump start and make the first day back less stressful. Our high school was sprawling, and we needed to map out when we would be able to see each other throughout the day.

"Ghost would be rolling in his grave if he had one," Bailey said after we passed the twentieth student none of us knew wearing a black ribbon tied around their wrists.

Apparently, they gave them out at the memorial.

"Don't you have to know someone before you can remember them?" I asked loudly as another student walked by. It obviously didn't register what I was talking about, since chances were they didn't know me either, but it still felt good.

Ghost would have scoffed at the idea of having a cheerleader-and-tears themed funeral, though he would have found the humor in it.

We all did some sort of exercise or athletic activity, but early on, we all found common interest in not making everything a competition. And at our school, cheerleading definitely fell under the competition umbrella. I think that was what we all loved about playing D&D and other RPG campaigns. We all got to work together, not against each other.

Except for the dungeon master, of course. He was usually out to ruin our lives. But we loved Bailey anyway.

"I kinda wish we had a place to visit him though," said Bailey. "Like a grave."

I gave Bailey a side hug, followed by a quick rap of his shin with my cane.

"Ow!"

"He's missing, not gone. And I'm going to figure out what happened to him, with or without you two," I said, standing up straight. Though honestly, if either of them abandoned me, I would probably collapse in on myself like a dying star.

"All right, all right," Corrin said. "But for now, let's just hope your third period is closer than your first and second. Because at this rate, you're going to be late to every single class."

"I have a doctor's note, remember," I said smugly, giving my cane a twirl that hit a sophomore.

"Hey!" the kid shouted, looking aghast.

"You're fine," I shot back and turned to my friends, with my cheeks reddening. "We gotta go. I want to get this run-through over with."

We finished walking our schedules and decided to head to the bookshop to pick up the novels we'd need for the semester's English class and to add to Corrin's ever-growing pile of books she owned. I had my own tiny library, but Corrin's was practically half her bedroom. The only other person I knew who had as many books as her was Ghost.

"I wonder what Ghost's folks are doing with his books?" I mused aloud as we got out of the car and walked to the bookshop.

The square where the shop was located was quaint, well lit, and crowded with folks doing back-to-school shopping and other regular Friday night things.

"They actually offered his books to me," Corrin answered quietly.

"Oh, really?" Bailey asked, "Did you take them?"

"A few," she said. "It felt rude not to. But also, he has a ton of books, and my parents might kill me if I tried to bring them all home."

"When were you over there?" I hadn't been to see Ghost's folks since I'd gotten home, mostly because I kept remembering at times that were not appropriate, such as right now.

"I try to pop by every week or so," Corrin said.

"Could I go with you next time?" I asked.

"Of course," she said, smiling at me. "They'd like that."

We got to the cafe side of the bookshop and made our way to a table by the window.

"It's my turn. I'll grab the drinks." Bailey made his way to the counter. We'd all pretty much settled on our favorites, and since we almost always got them together, it made it simpler to just take turns ordering.

"Hello to the two loveliest ladies in my life," Pacey said and pulled up a chair.

"Hi!" I said, smiling at them and scooching over to make room. "How are we supposed to survive this year without you?"

"Honestly, I doubt you'll manage," they said, patting my hand. "But I'm sure you'll do your best."

"Ha, thanks for that, not condescending at all." I rolled my eyes.

Bailey came over and passed our drinks around. A chai latte for Corrin, some sort of mocha coffee thing with lots of whipped cream for Pacey, un-sweet iced tea for Bailey, and a plain latte for me.

"Cheers to back to school," Corrin said, holding up her big, white coffee mug.

"To graduating," I chimed in.

"To senioritis," Bailey said.

"To us," added Pacey.

We clinked our mugs together, spilling more than a little. I wasn't sure what the year would bring, but I knew together we'd get through whatever senior year threw at us.

Chapter 5

It was one of the final days before the fall semester started, and I swung by the bookshop cafe and picked up a chai latte for Corrin, who was working at the art supply shop around the corner from the community fridge.

All three were within walking distance of my house and each other, which was convenient since I technically couldn't ride my bike for now, though honestly, the rate at which I tend to just bump into stuff out of habit even before I got hurt made me wonder what even was the point and would anyone notice.

The building was old and almost as long as half the block, with gigantic murals painted on both sides. They changed out every couple of years, and right now, there was a giant fox that ran along the entire length of one side, trailed by swirls of browns and yellows and whites, like it was running at top speed. Another read "Black Lives Matter" with a giant rainbow background that reached to the roof.

Not having my bike was working out, though, because no way could I have balanced both the steaming to-go cups on my Schwinn. It was hard enough doing it with my cane in one hand, but I managed. Sugar cookies and cane slung under my arm, I pushed through the old glass door at the art shop.

The bell above the entrance jingled a cheerful hello, and Corrin poked her head from behind the counter.

"Oh, hey, Chuck. I didn't expect you." She wiped her hands on the dark blue apron she always wore at work when she was applying gesso to canvases. She had just a tiny smudge of paint on her smooth, round cheek, and if my hands hadn't been totally burdened with goodies from the coffee shop, I might have been tempted to wipe it off.

"I needed some school supplies," I said, looking around and nodding toward the bin of erasers in the pencil area. "Do you happen to have any erasers shaped like zoo animals or snack foods?"

"Sorry," she said, coming around to grab the drinks, "We're fresh out, but the elementary school down the street is having a book fair in October."

"You actually know that, don't you?" I said, laughing.

"Of course. I wouldn't miss it. It's the main reason I still babysit Mrs. Snider's kids, so she'll let me in."

"The chai is for you." I shook my head in amusement and nodded at the drinks she was balancing.

"Well, come on then. I guess I'll let you hang out for a bit," she said, smiling.

We made our way to the tall, wooden stools behind the ancient counter. My parents had both come to this art shop when they were in college, and it had been in Tulsa for as long as pretty much anyone could remember. Okay, since 1952. Which was still a really long time ago.

I liked the feeling of running my fingers over the names carved into the back edge of the counter, from decades of people working the cash register.

Corrin sipped at her chai and did that thing where she closed her eyes and did a tiny little sigh when she was totally satisfied with something. Her chin tilted up just a smidge, and the little muscle behind her jaw moved a bit as she smiled.

"Thank you," she said and set the drink on the counter then got working on sorting items stashed in bins behind the checkout area. One thing I really admired about Corrin was she never stopped working, unless it was time to relax. I wished I had half the focus, though somehow, I ended up organizing an entire box of random colored pencils before I finished my drink.

She was basically a delegation wizard. I didn't even know how I got started on the project, but she gave me a "gold star" for effort.

"So, what else are you going to get up to today?" she asked.

The bell on the door jangled again.

"Oop, hold that thought," she said and got up to help the customer who had just come in. He was an older gentleman I recognized, and he nodded at me as they passed.

The two of them wandered off toward another part of the store. The building was rather maze-like. At some point in the sixties, they'd bought both of the warehouses on either side of the middle store front, so even I hadn't seen all of it. I made a mental note to look up what the other buildings had originally been but forgot by the time I picked up my to search for it online. ADHD is fun.

It was also fun to wander around and look at the years of random art that patrons had donated. So, no telling exactly where Corrin and the customer had gone or how long it would be until she was back.

I started scrolling through my phone, ogling alien shit as usual, when the bell went off again.

When I looked up, I knew I was looking at something alien in real life.

Ever since my accident, and—to be honest, even a while before then—I was keeping an eye out for otherworldly signs.

Sure, this thing didn't have antennae or a green tail or whatever, but it was off somehow. There was a subtle shimmer just underneath its skin, and I closed my eyes and took a deep breath, wondering if it would talk to me and if I would have a panic attack first.

In through the nose, out through the mouth.

In through the nose, out through the mouth.

Three times.

When I opened my eyes, it was standing right at the counter.

I couldn't help it. I leaned back, and I'm sure my face made a grimace. I hoped it understood resting awkward face was a typical human thing because that was for sure how I looked.

It was looking at me, with its blue eyes, blonde hair, and a Nirvana T-shirt that I wanted to believe was just a Walmart knockoff but looked vintage. So that meant it was probably around my age and had at least one really cool parent.

"Can I...help...you?" I asked, realizing too late that I was speaking like an annoying American on vacation in a foreign country.

"Bring me the magnets," it said, pulling its hair into a messy bun on top of its head and taking what looked like a cell phone out of its back pocket.

"The magnets?" I asked, confused.

Its jaw clenched, and under its skin, there was what looked like a shimmer again.

"Yes, magnets," it repeated, eyes flashing from blue to purple and back again. The blue was a quite enchanting shade. The purple gave me chills. Though maybe it was just the light coming in from the stained-glass pieces in the huge front windows.

"Oh...kay." I grabbed my cane and backed away. "I'll be right back with your...magnets..."

I hurried through the maze of matting supplies and canvases until I found Corrin. I tapped her on the arm, interrupting her conversation with the older customer.

"Hey, Chuck, I'm working. I'm sorry, sir, one second," she said, giving me a 'what the heck are you doing' look. "Why are you out of breath? Do you need to sit down?"

"There's a thing here, an alien, asking for its magnets," I said, giving her a meaningful look. Fully raised eyebrows, head tilted and everything.

"Chuck," she said, putting her hands on my shoulders and looking at me with her brown eyes, "what are you talking about? Do you need some water?"

Inclining my head toward the front of the store, I gave her another loaded look and directed my gaze at the thing waiting at the counter.

"Okay, gotcha," Corrin said, "even if you did all this really weirdly." She moved her hands off my shoulders, and I was briefly sad about it. She smiled at the man looking through the tubes of watercolors. "Sir, I'll be right back to help you if you need anything, just going to check this customer out really quickly."

Then Corrin walked right up to the counter, grabbed a box from under it, and handed it to the thing that was obviously an alien across from her and rang it up.

"That's gonna be $37.50 today, Dora," Corrin said, smiling.

"Thank you," said the so-called Dora. "Can you all send me a text or email when you get the rest in?" it asked after scooping up the receipt and box.

"Sure thing, see ya next time," Corrin said.

And it went out the door, turning and waving with only its fingers on the way out.

Even though I was already worn out from walking so far that day, I grabbed my cane and made for the door.

"Bye, Corrin!" I said as I rushed out of the store.

"Wait, Chuck, where are you going?"

"I'm gonna follow it," I said then added, "I'll see you later."

"Okay," Corrin said with furrowed brows. As I hurried out the door, she called after me, "Text me when you get home. I don't care if I sound like a concerned auntie. And be safe!"

At first, I wasn't sure if I was going to keep up with whatever it was, but turned out it was on foot and not in a tremendous rush. Several times, it stopped and took selfies in front of a few of the cooler murals in the area, and I mean, I could relate.

We turned off the main square and were making our way down a neighborhood street that I wasn't super familiar with. I was keeping pace with the Dora, though I wasn't sure how, since my mobility was below par.

Then it spun around and took several steps toward me.

"I knew you were following me!" the Dora said and pointed a finger at me with a smirk on its face.

An uncanny shudder ran down my spine.

Oh, that was how. It was *letting* me keep up.

"I come in peace." I held my left arm up, my right one planted firmly on my cane.

Turned out the Dora was a nonviolent but also humorless alien type, who waved at me in a snarky, open-hand, twirly-fingers type of way again.

"Didn't we have a class together last year?" it asked, its messy bun bobbing back and forth.

"I think I would remember that," I said. Though as usual, my brain was full of doubts, so it could have been a coin flip.

"I'll see you soon, Chuck," it said, and then it giggled and walked off about ten times faster than the average human ever could.

I'm talking next level, Olympic speed walker shit.

"I *knew* it," I said to myself then started walking back toward the square so I could finish up my errands.

The whole time I was cleaning out the community fridge, I kept looking around, expecting an alien to pop out any second. But the only folks I saw were a couple of fridge regulars and a parent pushing some kids in a stroller. Could have been aliens, but if so, a very mundane type.

I wasn't sure if it was better to be someone who saw aliens everywhere or didn't see them at all. Either way, I was tired. And I still had to get back home before meeting up with my pals later. I considered calling my parent, but I didn't want them to worry that I was wearing myself out before the school year had even started.

I ended up taking the bus, so it was an extra twenty minutes but worth it to sit and people watch. I was going to have to get my paranoia under control before the school year started, though, if I wanted to make it through.

Chapter 6

We spent a lot of those days digging around the internet and trying to find any information we could about portals.

Bailey went back to the quarry with me once, but we didn't see the portal appear while we were there. I knew it was hard for him to be back because my therapy had encouraged me to consider how the night had been for them, and I hadn't pressed any of them to go back with me after that initial visit.

We needed to find some clue about where Ghost had gone, and Pacey showed me the flyer for a UFO Convention that looked super official and was taking place in a hotel just outside of town the following weekend.

It took some begging. I wasn't above that. But my parents agreed I could go as long as Pacey's older sister drove us and we were back at a reasonable hour.

We bought tickets for the full Saturday event, and I had rarely been so excited to attend a con. We don't actually get a bunch of them in Oklahoma, believe it or not, so this one was not only timely but a real treat.

After checking in early the first day, we thanked the convention volunteer who was dressed like a Star Trek engineering officer. No one else was in cosplay, though, and if anything, it looked more like a business conference than one about extra-terrestrial life.

Taking a seat on a bench in the hallway of the medium-sized hotel, we studied the brochure and schedule handouts the ensign lookalike had handed us with our badges. There were events and panels scheduled for the whole day, and we circled the ones we were most interested in.

The alien abduction panel was the one we were most eager to attend, but it didn't start until after the lunch break, so we chose a few others in the meantime.

"Why don't we split up? There are two panels each hour, and we could get more info that way," Pacey suggested.

"Sure," I said sarcastically. "Why don't we just spend the whole morning having a low-key social anxiety panic attack and call your sister to pick me up early because I'm losing it?"

Pacey chuckled. "Well, Chuck, you do know yourself."

So, we stuck together.

The first panel we attended was all about how space travel requires way more powerful fuel sources than we have here on Earth. I almost fell asleep and spent most of the time on my phone, but Pacey was super engaged in what the speaker was babbling on about.

The second panel we attended was led by two "leading" UFO "scientist" women, and it addressed gender disparities in STEM, including the search for extraterrestrial life. But it managed to be trans exclusionary and laden with white feminism, so we left about fifteen minutes in, me "accidentally" banging my cane on almost every chair as we walked out.

The next panel, Radio Waves and You, was fine, though, and then we had a break for lunch. There was a small strip center down the block from the hotel, and we walked there along with a bunch of the other con attendees.

"So, what brings you here?" a plump middle-aged woman asked me. She was round-faced, and her badge bounced against her large chest as she walked with us and the other attendees to the limited choice of restaurants.

"Aliens?" I muttered because I was an awkward pigeon who came across as sarcastic even when I wasn't trying to be.

"Hi," Pacey said, reaching out their hand to shake the lady's. "I'm Pacey, they/them, and our friend got abducted, we think. Or possibly went through a portal willingly. We're not totally sure."

"Oh, you poor dears," she said, stopping and grabbing both our hands. "I'm Susan, she/her, and I'm so sorry for your loss."

"Thank you, ma'am." Pacey squeezed her hand back in a way that let go, rather than us being stuck holding her hand for the next twenty minutes, which was probably how it would have gone for me. "What brings you here?"

"Oh, I come every year," she said as we continued walking toward the shops. "My sister, she was abducted too."

"I'm really sorry to hear that," Pacey said. And they were. I wish I wasn't skeptical of people, but bless Pacey for being sincere in everything they do.

"You've come to the right place though," she said, gesturing to the group walking along the two-lane road. "If anyone can give you information about how to find your friend, this is the place."

We spent the whole lunch hour in the caring presence of a true Okie Alien aficionado and alllll of her friends.

Each of them had their own abduction story or expertise regarding the otherworldly, and a few seemed to have a lot of thoughts and knowledge about the Earth's government's involvement in alien issues. I began to stop being so skeptical and just tried to take in all their stories and insights.

Pacey and I ended up following Susan and her group to a sandwich shop that did not disappoint. There weren't many menu options, but the subs we got were amazing, and the fries were divine.

Susan let us know that she was "sensitive," whatever that meant. And we had a really entertaining lunch with her and her friends.

It was on our way back to see the alien abduction panel that things really got weird and her bringing that up made sense.

"Come with me," Susan whispered harshly and grabbed my arm. We were walking back to the convention hotel, and she pulled me into an honest-to-goodness alleyway.

"Let go of me!" I yelped, shrugging her off, but she tightened her grip and pulled me down so I was eye level with her.

"I have to show you something, Chuck," she said. Her voice had lost that sing-songy country vibe and was giving me stern teacher ones now.

She pulled her backpack around and unzipped the flap. Inside was a huge mess of wires and blinking lights and boxes. Susan grabbed a helmet lined with some sort of metal and slammed it on her head, then thrust the bag into my arms, and flipped a switch on one of the devices.

"Chuck?" said a voice.

"Ghost?" I asked, recognizing the voice coming through the machine even though it was not great reception.

"Yeah, it's me, dummy. You have to let me go. You have to stop searching."

"Un-fucking-likely," I scoffed.

"Dang it, Chuck, I don't have much time. Just stop calling attention to yourself. I know what I'm doing, and I have a plan. Let it alone."

"How are you doing this?" I wanted concrete answers. I wanted to know I wasn't hallucinating this. I wanted my best friend to be here and not just using whatever the heck this contraption was.

"That's not important," Ghost's voice said through Susan's machine.

"Why do you get to decide what's important?" I practically screamed. I didn't know if I wanted to cry or yell.

I looked around, and Susan was standing at the entrance to the alley, talking to Pacey. Her arms were on her hips, defiant, and her helmet planted firmly on her head.

"There are bigger things going on than just us, Chuck," Ghost said, but I could hear the reception waver.

"It's getting harder to hear you, Ghost!" I said, desperate for a few more minutes to chat with him. To ask him questions. To tell him he's a really great friend.

"Don't trust…" *static* "involved in…" *static* "…vernment…" *static* "message you…" *static.*

Then nothing.

Pacey looked at me, questioningly, from the end of the alley. Then, after glancing back, Susan let them through.

"Ghost was just talking to me," I said, my voice shaking.

Pacey whipped their head down to the device I held.

"He used whatever this is to do it," I said.

Susan walked up to us. She removed her helmet, putting it into the bag and zipping it up. "I'm gonna trust y'all not to mention this," she said. "And don't be asking me how we can call him back. I don't know, and I'm not trying to get involved with your friends, just get answers about my sister."

"Could I get a look at that?" Pacey asked, and I could tell they were itching to pull it apart to make their own.

"You're new around here" was all she said as she slung her bag onto her back. Then she gave us both a pat on the arms and said, "Enjoy the rest of the convention, you two."

Usually, I wouldn't want to be overheard talking about aliens, but we were smack dab in the middle of a crowd walking back to a UFO convention. They wouldn't mind. So, I filled Pacey in on what had just happened.

"What did he say?" Pacey asked as we made our way to the next panel.

"To stop looking for him," I said, grumpy. "How do you think he was able to do that?"

"I don't know, but it's the confirmation we need that he's out there and probably over his head in something big," Pacey said, and I could tell from their tone that they had approximately zero intention of listening to Ghost's "back off" message. Eager for more details, they asked, "What else did he say?"

"I don't know. It was hard to really hear. And we only spoke for a minute."

"I'm going to catch up with Susan and see if she'll give me more information on how that radio works," they said, and we walked quickly back to the convention.

We found her sitting in a panel about alien abductions and had to wait for the speakers to finish and then sit through the question-and-answer portion. It was quite concerning when the alien hunter panelist told someone who asked that there was nothing any of us could do to prevent an alien abduction. And the man was a self-trained martial artist, so I assumed he knew what he was talking about.

Afterward, Pacey caught up with Susan, and she was more than happy to give them her card, which only had a fully typed out URL for what she said cryptically was "a very helpful internet forum."

"Sort of feels like we passed a test?" I said as we waited for Pacey's sister in the parking lot once the convention wrapped up. They were already making a list of items they thought we'd need to make a device like Susan had, though where they thought we could get some of them was beyond me.

"Yeah, we are definitely on the right track," Pacey said, completely ignoring the fact that most of what Ghost said was to stay away.

But to be honest, I was fine with that attitude.

Chapter 7

"I'm telling you, the Dora is most definitely an alien," I said. "And even if Ghost said we should quit looking for him, it doesn't mean we have to. It's not like he's here to stop us."

I shook out our cloaks and laid out the various foam melee weapons while I filled Bailey in on the art shop incident and the UFO convention. Long broadswords, shorter dagger-sized ones, a few bows and arrows with foam balls at the tips.

"We probably won't use those today." Bailey adjusted his forest floor-colored pants and tightened the leather belt around his waist.

"Are you sure?" I looked somewhat forlornly at the weapons. "My PT said I was good to wail on you all."

He pulled out his campaign maps from his most prized possession. Bailey had decorated the outside of a satchel with winding vines and various poisonous flowers carved into the treated leather.

All of us had tried out leatherworking, but Bailey had really taken to it.

"Okay." I shrugged and begrudgingly started putting the weapons that would fit back into the duffle bag.

We'd used an enormous old chest I had picked up at an estate sale for a while, but it just wasn't practical to haul back and forth from house to park to woods to house again.

"It was just so bizarre," I was saying when Corrin rolled into the park on her skates. They were the equivalent to Bailey's bag on the pride-and-joy scale. Hers were purple with teal laces and magenta stitching. She wore them any time she could and had gotten super good at skating over the last year.

"What was so bizarre?" She sat on the park bench, took off her skates, and swapped them for the boots she had looped around her neck by the laces.

I missed skating so badly. Earbuds in, wind in my hair, falling over a lot. It was one of the eight trillion things that I was having to get used to, but at least I could start riding my bike so long as I don't push it too hard.

"The Dora alien," I said. "And the message from Ghost."

Corrin paused, unlacing her skates, and looked up at me. "Dora is a regular at the art shop, Chuck. She just wanted some magnets."

"I saw what I saw." I shrugged.

"She's literally a student at our school," Corrin insisted.

"That does not mean it's not from another planet. I'm telling you, something is going on."

"I'm pretty sure she's on student council. Aliens would not be on student council." She shook her head at me.

"I beg to differ. That is *exactly* where they would want to be. A place of power where they also blend in? It's a perfect cover."

"I think you're kinda obsessing about Dora."

"Can we not with the alien stuff today, please? I'm really wanting to get going on this story." Bailey crossed his arms and raised his eyebrows at me.

"I'm literally always with the alien stuff," I countered.

"Oh, Pacey just texted and said they can't make it. Sorry, Bailey." Corrin finished lacing up her boots.

"Dang it!" Bailey yelled, startling us both. He slammed his map folder together and shoved it into his satchel. "Like, are we ever even going to play anymore?"

"They're working on something from the convention, I guess?" Corrin said, sort of apologizing.

He was angry, red faced, and frustrated. All signs that something was bothering him.

"Sorry, Bailey, it's not like I *wanted* to skip a bunch of sessions," I said, trying to lighten the mood. But it didn't work.

"Obviously, I know that Chuck." He grabbed the duffle bag I was loading out of my hands. "I'm just gonna go, okay? Everyone has other"—he gestured around with his hands—"more important stuff."

"We could play something else," Corrin started.

But Bailey cut her off. "No, it's whatever. I'm heading home."

He grabbed his bike and, tossing the bag across his chest, he took off before either of us could really respond. We watched him go, pedaling quickly for someone balancing so much gear. I thought it might be fun to get a little wagon for him to attach to the back of his bike for his birthday.

"What's that about?" I asked Corrin, after he'd disappeared through the parking lot.

"He's been like this all summer. Even when it was just me and Pacey. If anything got in the way, he'd get upset. I think maybe he's just coping weirdly?"

"And what important stuff? Everything we do is with him." I watched as Bailey pedaled out of the park.

"That might be part of the problem, especially since half of us keep flaking," she said. I protested, but she held up her hand. "I obviously don't think you're 'flaking,' but that may be how it feels for Bailey."

I thought about that for a minute, but I wasn't sure what I could do to help make Bailey feel better. It wasn't like I could have been there for him more the past couple of months.

Corrin started lacing her skates back up. "Guess I'll head home. I need to get some of my AP English reading out of the way."

"Me too," I said. "Mind if I tag along?"

"Nope, come on then." She reached her hand out to get some help standing up.

As I grabbed hold and pulled her to her feet, it was one of those *I wish summer could be endless moments*, and I tried to do that thing my counselor was working on with me where I stay present. But as usual, my mind began to wander without asking for permission.

The day was seasonably warm, but the breeze was light and cooling. I walked my bike while Corrin skated in literal circles around me, neither of us wanting to actually read more of *The Great Gatsby*.

"I bet Ghost would have already finished all the summer reading," Corrin said as we walked past his house. Ghost was one of those students who was really good at school but also sort of loathed it most of the time.

There was a large flower bouquet visible through the huge bay windows across the front of his house, and I wondered whether my folks had sent some while I was in the hospital. They were probably pretty busy worrying about me.

"Pretty sure he finished all the summer reading before we got into first year," I said, chuckling. "What a nerd."

"The dorkiest."

"It was fantastic to hear his voice yesterday," I said.

We kept walking and skating quietly for a bit. Then Corrin spoke up. "I want to believe that Ghost is out there, doing some sort of adventure thing, Chuck, but that night was the worst of my life. And I don't want to fall apart if I let myself hope and then have to lose him again."

It took fighting every impulse in my direct brain-to-mouth channel to not fill the silence that followed her statement with a rebuttal and my own convictions that he's out there somewhere, but I managed to just nod. "Thank you for telling me that."

"What, no jokes?" She gave me a sidelong glance, and I think maybe she was smiling a bit.

"I mean, if you want to watch me put my foot in my mouth, I'd be happy to. It's just a little more difficult now that..." I gestured to my lower half and gave my cane a waggle.

That got a chuckle out of her, and it was that light airy one that meant she found something comforting, like that first bite of a freshly baked chocolate chip cookie or the smell of a Scholastic book fair.

When we got to her house, her mom said hey and did that grownup head-tilt, ultra-concerned thing, as she asked me how I was doing. I worried about the necks of all the adults in my life.

"Does this answer your question?" I twirled my cane around so fast it knocked into a cabinet and immediately fell back down to the ground, where I used my foot to roll across the handle and pick it up without having to bend down. "Tada?"

"Yeah, you're fine." She patted me on the shoulder.

Corrin and her mom look a lot alike. Dark brown skin and hair, wide eyes that looked like a Disney character when either of them wanted something from you, eyebrows knit together almost completely and their noses crinkled up when they found something annoying.

But while Mrs. Turner was quite tall and slender, Corrin was all curves and what she called chubby like her dad, though I would probably choose something more like voluptuous and then she would say I was being awkward and there was nothing wrong with being fat and that I shouldn't avoid saying something by covering up with SAT words.

To which I'd respond that I haven't even studied for the SAT, and she'd do that anger crinkle face at me.

"Let me know if you need anything," Mrs. Turner said and went back to the work she had spread out on the kitchen island. She had been an architect at a major firm for ages, but once she got a taste for working at home, she branched out on her own so their kitchen was always full of classical music and drawings of parks and libraries and houses.

"Will do. Thanks, Mom," Corrin said, and the two of us walked down the hallway to her room.

She had roomy, wooden bunk beds, even though she'd never had to share a room, and I was always jealous of them. She had curtained the bottom one off with a flowered sheet she'd sewn up, and she'd positioned a small writing desk against the window, which looked out on the gigantic oak trees that lined her street.

"I call top bunk!" I screamed, like I did every time, and she rifled through her book bag while I climbed up the wooden ladder.

She'd converted the top part of the bed into a cozy reading area and plastered every inch of the wall with pictures from magazines and old books. Everything from 80s' celebrities to cranes to random pumpkins. It was even encroaching on the ceiling, and if Corrin didn't get accepted into college somewhere far enough away to keep her from living at home, it might take over the entire room.

"I spy with my little eye, something green." I scooted over while she climbed up next to me and tossed me my copy of *The Great Gatsby*. I tried to convince her to just watch the movie, but she assured me it was garbage and we were better off plowing through this quote-unquote classic before college.

"Plus, we can compare it to *Their Eyes Were Watching God* by Zora Neil Hurston for our essay that's due a few weeks from now," she said. I started to counter this plan, but she waved me off. "I already got the okay from Ms. Wann to do the same book as you. Pretty sure the teachers are going to do whatever you ask this year."

"That would be a pleasant change of pace."

"We're on page forty-two, right?" Corrin said, and I nodded. We took turns reading until we needed a break from all the literary decadence, and I texted my folks, letting them know where I was and that Mrs. Turner was feeding me dinner.

My mom let me know I was supposed to wait for one of them to get a ride instead of biking, and that was fine with me because I was beat, even if I'd never admit it.

After dinner, we read a few more pages to get to the end of a chapter then decided to go outside and enjoy the air before I had to leave.

"Pacey really thinks you're right, you know," Corrin said as we sat on her big, wooden porch steps, waiting for my parent to come get me. There were fireflies dotting her yard, blinking in and out, and the moon was a crescent sliver of a thumbnail pressed into the velvety black sky.

"But you don't?" I took a sip of the warm oolong tea we'd made and thought about what a waste of a life everyone in *The Great Gatsby* had and how selfish they all were. I wanted to make something bigger for myself, and I wanted to do it with my friends.

But it was hard to be around people who you suspect think you might be making stuff up in your own head. It was easy to get caught in a paranoid loop.

"I'm not sure," she said, honesty apparent in the contemplative way she was holding her mug. "Though hearing what you said happened yesterday is definitely making me feel like the whole situation is more urgent."

"Sometimes I feel like Bilbo at the beginning of *Fellowship* when he's like super adamant about going to see the mountains again."

"What do you mean?"

"I know there's something going on. And I know what I saw wasn't Earthly, but I don't know how to tell people how much I want it to be true without coming across as totally bonkers. I don't want to be some desperate adventure maker-upper."

She laughed. "You don't want to be Don Quixote?"

"Yes! Exactly."

"Well, even he had Sancho Panza and that donkey."

"Sure, but even they didn't believe him," I said, trying not to be distressed. I needed us to do whatever this was together. I was so used to Ghost, who would leap with me at any whim either of us had.

"That definitely wasn't the point of the friendships in the book though. They had adventures, no matter what each person was seeing or how their interpretations and experiences were different." Corrin placed her hand on my slumped shoulder.

The low lights from my parent's car swung around the corner and came up the short driveway.

"So, you're saying you're my donkey?" I got up and dusted my pants off.

"Sure, Chuck, I'll be your donkey." She walked me to the car and opened it as I got in. "Hi, Nice to see you both." She nodded to my parent and my little brother in the back seat.

"Hi, Corrin." Arty screeched from his booster seat.

"Okay, but can I say 'Donkey' like Shrek does every time I address you?" I asked.

"Good night, Chuck," she said with a smile and closed the door behind me. "I'll see you tomorrow," she added through the closed window.

"Get your reading done, sweetheart?" my parent asked as we pulled away.

"No, but we made a lot of progress."

"Do you want to play video games with me when we get home?" Arty asked.

"Only if you're ready to be decimated at Mario Kart."

"You're on," he said, kicking the back of my seat. "And it's my turn to pick the music!" So, we listened to the Adam West *Batman* theme song on repeat for the blessedly short drive.

Chapter 8

The first day back in school went about how I expected. Everyone, especially the people who never even glanced at me before, decided it was their mission to be up in my business. It was all in stares and whispers though. Never right to my face, of course, which made it even worse.

Not just students either, but the teachers were just as gossipy. I would have worried that my cheeks were going to catch fire, but that ship sailed about twelve minutes into first period when the Spanish teacher gave us a writing prompt that was "Write about the most interesting thing that happened to you this summer," and, no exaggeration, every single kid turned in their seat to look at me.

They couldn't have timed it better if they'd tried.

If the teacher made us read ours aloud, I was planning to climb out a window and just wait until the fire department arrived or I perished from stressful attention.

"How's it going?" I asked the group via text between second and third period.

Corrin immediately replied with a string of poop and fire emojis, and Bailey just added a finger pointing to what Corrin sent in agreement. No word from Pacey, but they're probably in the middle of a recorded seminar.

"Lunch in the usual?" Corrin texted back.

"Heck yeah," I replied.

Bailey chimed in with a thumbs-up emoji.

I wondered briefly if we should start a second chat without Pacey for when we're doing at school stuff, but they could always mute us during school if they wanted. They always let us know how they really felt eventually. I made a mental note to ask ahead of time. Then my brain reminded itself that unless I write something down, there's no hope in my remembering it, and at that point, I assumed it wasn't important.

Thankfully, it was time for weightlifting, and I knew I wouldn't have to think about other students much for the next hour.

Yes, I loved weightlifting class. I thought about taking track again this semester as well. It always surprised coaches when they saw me slink in with my black hoodies and Totoro backpack, then found out I was actually pretty strong, and fast.

Well, not quite so fast anymore. But the physical therapy all summer had kept me relatively fit, especially my upper body. My back was, unfortunately, going to be a problem for the rest of my life, but conditioning was always a good thing to keep up with. And my physical therapist told me I shouldn't overexert myself. Plus my therapist was worried my being slower so much more than I'm used to would bum me out.

It was true I wouldn't ever make a hurdle jumping team, but I wanted to get back to at least jogging.

It was Ghost who first got all of us to take more than Fitness for Beginners to fulfill our PE requirements.

"Think of how we could up our LARP game," he'd said the summer before first year.

We'd been watching *The Empire Strikes Back* for the seven hundredth time.

That summer was scorching, and Ghost's mom had let us all go in on an above-ground pool, so long as we were the ones to keep it maintained. Bailey and Corrin had rigged up a projector so we could swim in the four feet of water and marathon movies. At the peak of the heat wave, we'd tossed full bags of ice into the water with us to cool it down.

Mosquitoes couldn't eat you alive if you were mostly underwater, and we saved a lot of money by not going to the actual theater as often as we would have. It's really hard to beat air conditioning, but you can only watch the new *Spiderman* movie so many times.

We were at the part where Yoda is training Luke on Dagobah. He was dressed like Sarah Connor at the start of *Terminator 2: Judgment Day*, and Pacey pointed out how they were both equally hot buffing-up montages.

To which Corrin immediately scoffed, "Sarah Connor is the original hot mom. Do not compare her to that whiny little man child."

"Sarah Connor is how I knew I was queer," I said, paddling around with my hands trailing lazily in the water. "And Lando Calrissian is how I knew I was bi."

"Princess Leia solidified my hetero-normative preferences," Bailey said, waggling his eyes at the princess on the screen. "In case y'all didn't know, pretty sure I'm straight."

"Yeah, she's my pick too," Corrin added.

"Yoda is how I knew I was ace?" Pacey said. The question inflection they exaggerated at the end, and the gigantic shrug of their shoulders had us all rolling.

"What does that even mean?" I asked, giggling.

"Exactly." Pacey nodded and pointed their fingers sagely.

"Well, I'm solidly undecided," Ghost said. "But as I was saying, being fit is good for all orientations."

I laughed. "That is not what you were saying."

"No, but it makes sense now that I think about it." He splashed me. Before long, he had us convinced to work toward our own training montage.

It worked too. After actually doing some workouts that summer, we all noticed it was more fun to do melee fights and role play outside. It started with mostly swimming in circles in the pool pretending to be water benders like in *Avatar: The Last Airbender.*

We got really into rock climbing for a while. We spent a summer being rock gym rats, and Corrin even convinced us to all choose a different color and stick to wearing just that so she could live out her Power Rangers fantasies. The equipment was too expensive to buy ourselves, but we could rent everything at the gym with our memberships.

One day Pacey fell though. They hadn't clipped in frequently enough, and Ghost wasn't paying as close attention as he should have been.

Pacey slipped and was in the air for fifteen feet maybe?

But from the ground, it looked like they were falling for a year. One of those slow-motion life moments.

That was how it felt when I fell too but even longer. I tried to tell them all when I woke up that it was like in that classic movie *Contact*, where she just dropped for like a second but then was gone eighteen hours. I just wished I had Ghost to talk to about it. He'd get what I was saying, even if I didn't totally know how to say it.

That was what I'd been thinking about when the coach said it was time to pack up for the day. I threw on some deodorant and quickly changed clothes in the locker room. People who can shower in a locker room full of other people are not who I was born to be. Tomorrow, I would add some shampoo and soap to my gym locker because I realized I could us the disabled bathroom. Perhaps I would not have to go through the second half of my day smelling quite so ripe.

When I closed my gym cubby door, the Dora was standing right behind it.

I let out a little yip and jumped back.

"Excuse me, sorry. This is my locker." It pointed to the one next to mine.

"I didn't see you there," I said, eyes narrowing with suspicion.

It said nothing and swept its long, blonde hair up into another perfect messy bun and pulled its over-sized Swifty cardigan off, reaching for its small pile of gym clothes.

I backed up and shut my locker with my cane once I was a safe distance away.

"Are you okay?" It sounded like it was asking genuinely. Not like everyone else who already knew the rumor-fueled details about what was going on in my life but felt obligated to ask. "Do I scare you?"

Now, *that* question really took me by surprise.

"Do you come in peace?" I asked.

It laughed and popped its shoes into the locker and pulled out a pair of pristine white trainers. They had either never been worn or were made of some alien, future, smudge-free fabric.

"Do you want me to come in peace?"

Oh my god, was the Dora flirting with me right now? What was happening?

Just then I swear, between blinks, its face changed, and it was like looking into a mirror. When I blinked again, it was looking up at me with cartoon fawn eyes only a foot away and a smile that could only be described as coy.

I said bye and got out of the locker room as fast as I could.

It took me a full ten minutes to get to the grassy slope where we always ate, and by the time I arrived, Bailey and Corrin were halfway through their lunches. We'd eaten here every day since first year. Ghost had scouted it out for its general obscurity, proximity to the library, and wide view of the rest of the quad. I plopped down next to them and pulled out my salad. I was famished and only had a few minutes to eat.

"So, I think we should eat closer to the gym." Corrin handed me a sweet tea dripping with condensation.

I nodded in thanks, my mouth full of rock-hard croutons.

"No, it's okay," I said after swallowing.

"We don't mind," Bailey said.

"I know, but I don't want to be the reason we have to change," I said then realized what a silly thing that was to say. Everything had changed already.

No Pacey at school.

No Ghost at all.

Aliens. I refused to be convinced otherwise.

I had permanent nerve damage and carried around a badass, amber-colored cane.

And who knew what else was coming down the line.

I looked down at my salad, focusing on the cucumbers before I teared up.

"We already talked about it, and we decided the library works better anyway," said Corrin. "Since I'm a library aide this year, Mrs. Baker said we could use one of the assistant's tables as long as it's just the three of us."

"Has anyone ever told you that you're kinda bossy?" I stabbed at a tomato, but my heart wasn't in it, so it popped out of the plastic container and rolled down the slope.

"Be free, tomato," I whispered after it.

"What I heard you say was 'thanks for looking out, friend.'" She handed me one of those brown napkins that felt like sandpaper.

"Thanks for looking out, friend," I repeated. "But I'm not actually crying."

"It's for the Ranch Dressing." She rolled her eyes at me, pointing to the side of my mouth. "You're my favorite mess, by the way."

"And you're my favorite dumpster fire."

"*Anyway*, I'm here too," said Bailey.

To be honest, I *had* kind of forgotten he was there for a second. Stupid gay heart. "Has anyone heard from Pacey today? Also, I had another encounter with the Dora."

"You have *got* to stop calling her that, Chuck. She has a name, and it's Dora. Just Dora, no 'the.'" Corrin finished up her chicken salad wrap and wadded up the paper.

"I'm telling y'all, it is a shapeshifter."

"I thought you said she was an alien," Bailey said, clearly annoyed at me as a general human presence in his life.

"Right, a shapeshifter alien. Don't you think it's weird that suddenly it keeps showing up everywhere I am?"

"You mean, at school?" Corrin asked, finishing up her salad and standing to take her trash to the bin. "You think it's weird that a student would show up at school? A student who goes here, to this school?"

"Well, not when you put it that way," I said. "Seriously, though, what's up with Pacey?"

"I'm not sure, but I haven't heard from them either," Bailey said. "And I am seriously wanting to start role playing again. This is getting ridiculous."

"I have to get to class, but if either of you hears from them, let the others know, okay?" Corrin gathered up the rest of the trash and walked it to the big bin by the sidewalk.

"They're probably just working on that radio device thingy." I hoped that was the case. "But of course, if anyone hears from them, we'll text."

We all agreed and headed to our next classes. I noticed they'd given us a lot longer to make it than usual. I wish everyone else made those little accommodations without making it such a fuss. But that was why my friends were the best. We were just down a few of our regular numbers for now.

It was much harder to concentrate on school than usual since I kept checking my phone every few minutes. It wasn't just the lack of Pacey in the desks next to mine. It was their lack of even a random hang-in-there-cat meme that had me on edge. Where was Pacey?

Chapter 9

"**S**eriously, has anyone heard from Pacey?" Bailey asked, exasperated.

"Not since yesterday? Maybe?" Corrin said.

We were all in Bailey's basement, reviewing our character sheets and the table for the night's campaign. Both Corrin and I wanted to start a new one, but Bailey insisted on wrapping this campaign up with one last session.

His exact words were, "We can make it a sendoff for Ghost."

So, we obviously couldn't argue with that.

We were all coping in our own way, and Bailey's was to create an elaborate funeral procession story line for Ghost's rogue. I was sure it would have been very touching if we could have gotten it started, but Pacey was running late. Very late. And it was really unlike them.

"This is all really impressive, Bailey," I said.

He'd decorated the basement even more than usual and had the black cult robes ready to go. I wasted no time, pulling mine on immediately. We used them for tons of stuff, but "cult robes" never lost the ring it had to it.

Bailey had draped flowers from the ceiling above the table, and candles were lit everywhere, most in tall, brass holders. I was pretty sure I recognized most of the flowers as leftover decorations from his oldest sister's backyard wedding last year, but regardless, they were lovely.

He'd painted an entire crypt map on heavy paper to go with the end of the campaign. There were so many details that showed off his impressive watercolor skills. His art teacher had actually given him the go-ahead to focus on maps for his senior portfolio.

"I agree. It's really lovely," Corrin added.

"Thank you," he said, but he was pacing around, clearly frustrated and trying to shake it off.

"I'll go upstairs and try calling them again," I said. There was absolutely zero reception in Bailey's basement, which was fine since it was usually the five of us and if one of our parents needed to get in touch, they knew to call Bailey's family's landline.

Yes. Landline. It's a thing where you talk on a phone that is tethered to the wall by a twisty cord.

I scrolled through all our chats, and it looked like Pacey had left us on read like a day and a half ago.

Then nothing.

This wasn't like them at all.

I called their number for the third time that day and still no answer, but this time the phone didn't even ring, just went straight to voicemail. Then I called their parent's house and still nothing.

"Hey, y'all, I think we should go over there to check on them," I hollered from the top of the basement stairs.

Corrin and Bailey peered up at me from the bottom. Both were wearing their black hoods and, in the candlelight, totally looked like clerics. I was into it.

"Okay fine," Corrin said and, after quickly circling the room to extinguish the candles, they both grabbed their backpacks and headed upstairs to join me.

"Mom, we're going to Pacey's. We'll be right back!" Bailey yelled through the house as we headed out the door.

The walk to Pacey's house didn't take long, and we took the shortcut through the nature park. We'd spent countless hours trudging through here, and all three of us knew the paths, even without flashlights. Even though I had to pick my way a tad slower than on previous treks, we made it to their back fence swiftly.

Even in the nature park, we weren't super far away from civilization. At least a bit of light from streetlamps illuminated most of the park's edges, and there was a quarter moon lighting things up as well.

When we got there, though, things felt strange.

"I've got a bad feeling about this," Corrin said unironically.

Everything felt too silent, the air too still.

"Me too," I said.

The entire house was lit up. Bright lights streamed from every window, and there were figures moving around behind the curtains. Tall, slender shapes passed by the windows and the glass door downstairs. We could see several moving around in Pacey's room as well.

"What is going on?" Corrin whispered.

"I do not know," said Bailey.

Just then, something jerked back on my robe, and I stumbled backward away from the house.

"Ah!" I shouted, as a hand clamped over my mouth.

"Shh," Pacey said sharply, pinching my lips together with their fingers.

71

Bailey and Corrin spun around, startled, but kept from yelping like I did. Not sure how they managed it because the moment was startling in the least.

"Pacey, what is happening?" Bailey asked in an urgent but hushed voice.

"Come with me and keep low and for the love of everything, be quiet, Chuck," they whispered and took off at a low run back into the nature park.

"Hey what about them," I pointed to Corrin and Bailey who simultaneously put their fingers to their lips and shushed me.

"Fine" I mouthed.

We moved quickly and quietly for a few minutes until we arrived at the empty oil drum. When we'd started using it as a club house in middle school, our guess was it had been abandoned ages ago, and when they created the nature preserve, no one had the funds or motivation to move the thing since it was gigantic and heavy and in the middle of a ton of trees that had grown around it.

Cylindrical and rusted out on both ends, the space had always been great for hanging out in or waiting out the occasional thunderstorm. Green moss had grown up over the sides, and years of leaves had piled against the base, so it made a sturdy and cozy hideout.

It did, however, flood, when it rained enough, so definitely not a great place to store stuff on the ground, which we found out the hard way.

R.I.P. my *Miles Morales* comic collection.

"Okay, what in the world is happening right now?" Corrin said as soon as Pacey ushered us all in.

They crouched down and gestured for us to follow. Corrin turned on her phone flashlight and laid it on one of the small, wooden tables we'd thrown together, so we were all illuminated.

"Who were those people?"

"Where have you been?"

"Why are you dressed like Rambo?"

"Chill out, you three. We don't have much time." Pacey smoothed their dark hair out of their eyes and took a deep breath. We all waited impatiently.

"We were right." They looked at me, eyes wide and legit glowing with excitement.

"About?" Corrin prompted.

"All of it. There are definitely aliens, and Ghost is with some of them. And I found our proof."

Bailey sighed audibly, and Corrin pinched the bridge of her nose with her fingers.

"You did?" I ask excitedly, leaning closer.

"Yes, but I can't exactly show you right now," they said.

At this, Bailey and Corrin both groaned.

Pacey ignored them. "I made a modified version of the communicator Susan at the convention had, and I'm pretty sure it works."

"That is so cool!" I shouted.

All three shushed me.

"I mean, yay, go you," I stage-whispered.

"I'm close to getting it to work, but the FBI knows and also the Cralzod, and that's why they're searching my house. I have to go find a bit more proof, and I don't think anyone is happy with me snooping around so I'm gonna be on the run."

"You have to go…" Corrin asked, eyes wide. "On the run. From aliens. To find aliens?"

"To find Ghost," they said, eyes brimming with hopeful tears. "He's alive, and I know it. We have to find him."

I took a deep breath and looked at them. They were serious. I'd never seen them with this amount of determination. At least not since we gave jousting a go at the medieval faire a few years ago. That was something else.

"How do you know?" Bailey asked.

"While I was trying out frequencies, I got into a server that was actually part of the Cralzod's network. That's how I know they can shapeshift," Pacey said. I wished I could have a fraction of their computer skills. I still used two fingers to type.

"Whoa, next level," Bailey said, giving them a high five.

"Wait, what is a Cralzod?" Corrin interjected.

"An alien species that, from what I gather, is pretty focused on invading Earth and not in a copacetic way."

"Oh, that's not good," I said, knowing as I said it that it was obvious. But what else do you say to information so laden with cringe?

"Yeah, and also, they figured out what I was doing, hence the hurry."

"Are you sure you have to leave?" I ask. "Maybe the FBI—" I started, and they cut me off.

"Look. I'm not just tossing around conspiracy theories, and I really don't have time to explain all of this to you because I have to leave like yesterday," they said, taking off their backpack and rummaging through it. "Ghost is wrapped up in some major stuff, and I have to try to find him. I don't know who he's working with, but he might be in trouble, based on the bit of info I got."

"We'll go with you," I blurted out.

"That's really sweet, but no way. I'll be faster on my own, and we'd arouse way more suspicion if we all left at once. But I'll be in touch."

"How?" Bailey asked. Pacey threw him a quick glance.

"I'll contact you when I can," they said and pulled out a small cube-like device from their backpack, handing it to Bailey. It was about the size of a Rubik's Cube but had small wires and buttons all over it. Pacey was really getting good with tiny welds.

"Where's your phone?" Corrin asked.

"I destroyed it," they said, and Corrin nodded in approval.

"I knew you weren't just ignoring me," I said smugly.

They riffled through the pages in their composition book and ripped out several from the middle and thrust them at me.

"Find a place to hide these, separately, because I'm guessing they're going to come question you next," Pacey said. "Do not trust them. They might not actually be FBI agents."

"I wasn't planning on trusting them either way?" I said, because it felt like it sounded cool. I quickly glanced at the notebook pages, but the writing on it was in a code. Pacey was fantastic at codes, but they could also be a complicated pain in the neck.

"Are we supposed to know how to solve this?" Bailey asked, taking the sheets from me and handing me the cube, shining his cell phone light on them.

"You will eventually. But if I tell you now, I'm afraid the FBI might figure it out when they question you, and I need a head start."

"That sounds...ominous," I said. "But they'll never break me."

Corrin let out a sharp laugh.

"Hey!" I said, and she just shrugged.

"I'm sorry it has to be this quick, but I will find you and I will have answers," they said, pulling their backpack on and flipping open an honest-to-goodness compass. "If I don't come back, you all will have to figure it out and keep searching."

"Hang on a second!" Corrin said and opened her own backpack. After pulling out—I kid you not—*three* books, she found what she was looking for and handed Pacey a small, green canvas bag.

They looked at it but hesitated.

"I can't," Pacey said.

But Corrin shook her head and thrust the bundle into Pacey's hand. "It was your idea to make them in the first place,"

A few years ago, we'd gone on a survivalist kick, and Pacey had insisted we all put together go kits. Someone— definitely not me. I'm very responsible—had slowly used mine up over the years, and I'd never replenished things like the tissues, Band-Aids, and snacks. Those went first.

The bags were actually really efficient and had all sorts of helpful stuff. It was what happens when a bunch of kids got together to make a bag that would give you the highest chances of winning a competition where they dropped you in the forest. So, no Bowie knives, but like ponchos and other stuff our parents let us play with.

"You still carry that around?" I asked, surprised and also impressed.

"I use the sewing kit like twice a week." Corrin shrugged.

"Thank you, Corrin," Pacey said.

"You better make it back safely," she said, helping Pacey put it into their bag.

"Oh and here." I pulled out my wallet. "I have like—oh wow, sorry—twelve...no, thirteen dollars. You shouldn't use credit cards."

"Way ahead of you, pal." Pacey pocketed all the cash the three of us had on hand.

"What do we tell your parents?" Corrin asked.

"I told them I'd gotten into a really elite FBI computer camp and that the suits showing up was a test," Pacey said somewhat sheepishly. "I don't like lying to them, but this is important."

"We'll check on them, promise," I said

They smiled at me. "I know you will."

Then, with quick hugs all around, they left as suddenly as they'd shown up.

"What the actual shipwreck was that?" Corrin asked as soon as Pacey had slipped out of sight into the now-creepy trees.

"Hopefully, this will explain some things." I clutched the cube and stared after Pacey in the dark.

Chapter 10

The "FBI," or at least something that looked a lot like a caricature FBI agent, came and talked to all of us over the next day or so. Each one was a tall, skinny, white dude in aviator glasses, which honestly made us more suspicious than Pacey's warnings had. My mom was really worried that the questioning was going to upset me, but since Pacey had given us a heads-up, the questioning itself wasn't too bad.

My other parent even piped in with, "Why is the FBI interested in a high school kid from Tulsa?"

Apparently, the answer was because of some really wild alien stuff. But also, nothing we were willing to answer in the detail they were looking for.

Why were we at the quarry?

"Hanging with friends."

How did I sustain my injuries?

"Doing stupid stuff with friends."

Where are my friends now?

"At their houses, I assume."

When was the last time I saw my friend?

"Which...one...?" I drew this last answer out with a raise of my eyebrows and an unblinking gaze I hoped was badass.

To which they must not have had an answer because they just said, "If you think of anything, let us know," and handed my folks a business card that looked so much like cheap ones you could get printed anywhere, I almost laughed.

Who or whatever they were, they were still watching us. I was sure of it. Though since it was mostly a feeling, I tried to act natural.

My parents insisted I go to some extra therapy sessions, which was fine with me. I really liked my therapist, and even though I couldn't tell her everything that happened, it was always good to talk about Ghost. And now Pacey.

Plus, I thought that the confusion I was feeling about everything that was happening was no less confusing than general teenager-ness, so even her most generic advice pertained.

Pacey had somehow convinced their parents that whatever they were up to was important enough to not talk to the potentially-fake FBI about because when I went to check on them, they were mostly worried that Pacey might fall behind on their online schoolwork while they were at "some special camp for computers." They actually brought it up like five times in the twenty minutes I was over there and asked me to remind them to keep up with their assignments.

"Thanks for checking on us, dear," their mom said. "They let us know that they'd be gone for a while."

"Just making sure you all were okay," I said.

"Of course, we're very proud that Pacey got into such a great computer camp. If they get in touch with you, will you let us know?" she asked, and I agreed.

I met up with Corrin and Bailey a half hour later. "Yeah, Pacey's folks are fine."

"Phew," Corrin said.

We wanted to keep an eye on them, to make sure they didn't get worried enough to start asking questions to the wrong people. Not that we had a full grasp on who that would be, but Pacey had emphasized caution.

"What else did they say?" Bailey asked.

"They acted like their primary concern was making sure they got their schoolwork turned in on time."

"I don't know if I'm jealous of how cool their parents are or stressed out about how cool they are. Does that make sense?" Corrin asked.

We were all sitting in the basement at Bailey's house, as usual. His mom had brought us a plate of pizza rolls, and we were munching on them. We wanted to have more sophisticated palates, but nothing beat some pizza rolls or a cup of ramen after a long day of not understanding where exactly your best friends had adventured off to without you and whether aliens were surrounding your planet.

Since minutes after Pacey had taken off, we'd been trying to sort through the notes they left to figure out how the cube worked and felt like we were getting nowhere. It seemed like a total red herring, and I was not enjoying being left behind while who knew what Pacey and Ghost were getting up to.

"Any luck?" I asked, and they both shook their heads.

We had a long list up on Bailey's white board of what the code wasn't. The list included Klingon, the Imperial Alphabet, and the Cylon alphabet from BSG. We had all decided it was most likely one purely from Pacey's imagination or based on an alien thing they hadn't shown any of us.

Which made it much more of a challenge, given our lack of a key or solid context. We assumed it was some sort of clue to get linked up with Pacey and/or Ghost.

But otherwise, nothing.

Nothing showed us any more information about how to read the notes. Not lemon juice, heat, light, dusting for prints, all things we'd learned about from Nancy Drew books we'd read growing up. If Encyclopedia Brown had tried it, we did too. And any googling we did about the cube just led down Star Trek Borg fan sites, which was less than helpful.

"Do you think Pacey was just messing with us?" I asked earnestly.

Bailey groaned.

"Let's get out of this basement," Corrin said, standing up and stretching.

"Sno Cones?" I suggested, and Bailey nodded in consent.

"No, I mean like actually out," Corrin said. "Of town. And not just to a UFO convention in Guthrie."

"Is there a convention this weekend?" I asked, perking up.

"No, Chuck. No," she said. "Let's go camping this weekend."

"I'm not sure if my folks will be up for me camping," Bailey said. Out of all of our parents, his had been keeping him closest since the night of the accident.

"I know, but this is school sponsored." Corrin, excited, pulled up the school website, where sure enough, there was a senior class camp-out that weekend. I normally wouldn't want to go to a school-sponsored event, but any sort of camping sounded good. And Bailey getting to go would be a bonus.

"What does it cost?" he asked.

"Nothing! It's in place of that Senior Sunrise thing that kids used to do where they'd pick a day senior year to stay up all night and watch the sunrise," Corrin said. "Parents got tired of how many kids would ditch the next day, so now it's school sponsored and always on a Friday." She had obviously been planning this speech and thought through any holes Bailey or his folks might find in the plan.

"I'm opposed on principle, because school-sponsored anything is against my vibes as a rebel," I said. "But if it means you can go, Bailey, let's do it."

"Who am I supposed to share a tent with?" Bailey looked at us like we had personally thrown his tent into the river.

"How about we all sleep out under the stars together, no tents?" I actually really enjoyed that idea.

"I'm pretty sure that's what everyone does anyway, because it makes it easier for the sponsors," Corrin added.

He looked at her and nodded. "Okay, fine, I'll ask, but if the two of you ditch me and end up in a tent, I'm going to be so angry."

"We probably wouldn't do that to you, Bailey." I said, smirking.

"Actually, I think I may know one or two people going." He sort of looked away from us.

"Ooo really?" I asked, taking the bait and waggling my eyebrows at him. "Any *particular* person we might know?"

"Ugh, leave me alone. I'm gonna go ask my folks so I can hopefully do something more productive than stare at nonsense with you two." Bailey got up and went upstairs, taking the steps two at a time. A few minutes later, he hollered down from the top step, "They said yes, and also, there are more pizza rolls."

Corrin grinned at me. "Looks like we get to start packing."

Chapter 11

The three of us took seats toward the back of the bus—but not so far back we might be mistaken for rascals—and had no trouble getting seats together. Not as many seniors had signed up for the overnight trip as expected, so none of the three chartered buses were full.

My guess was that some of the "cooler kids" were still planning to do an overnight and ditch day, but I was glad the three of us could go, whether or not there were faculty sponsors.

Bailey took out his D&D book to make notes, Corrin pulled out her Switch and started playing *Pokémon Snap*, and I pored over the notes Pacey had made for the umpteenth time. We'd left the cube stashed in the wheel well of Corrin's car where the spare tire was kept because it seemed risky to keep the cube and the notes together. We were getting pretty good at this whole secret quest thing.

"Is this seat taken?" a voice from out of nowhere asked. Okay, out of nowhere might not be totally accurate since we were on a bus full of students, but it startled me nonetheless.

"Gah!" I yelled and fumbled my notes, which spilled over Corrin and into the aisle.

Bailey looked at me like I was totally losing it and helped me scoop them up quickly. Where had the Dora come from so suddenly? Was I just that zoned into my notes?

I looked around, and half of the seats on all sides of us were empty.

"No, come sit," Corrin said, and the Dora took the seat directly in front of us. It turned around and immediately started talking to Corrin about the project it had needed the magnets for. Corrin gave me a *please try to act like a normal person for two minutes* look, and I swear it was like she knew I was still referring to the Dora as "the Dora" in my head.

Or did I say it out loud?

"It's sort of like a combination art and science installation," the Dora was saying.

"That sounds really cool." Corrin leaned forward in our seat and rested her chin on the back of the Dora's. Which didn't bother me like at all. It was fine.

"Yeah, I'm sort of trying to experiment with how we're drawn together by art and science and stuff."

I snorted because show off, much?

And Corrin straight up kicked me in the foot.

"It's coming up really soon," Corrin said. "Maybe you can both come to the opening." She looked at me and Bailey. That was when I noticed Bailey was just sitting quietly, blushing, and I swear, ogling the Dora.

"That would be"—the Dora paused for effect—"ahh-mazing!"

"I've never been to an art opening, I don't think." Bailey shifted forward with his elbows on his knees. If he leaned much further, he'd fall over.

Then who would people say is the clumsy one!

"They're great," Corrin said. "You can ask the artists about their work, and sometimes pieces are for sale. And there are almost always free snacks."

"Of course you would have been to art openings, Cor, what with working at the art shop and all." The Dora beamed at her.

"Good job piecing that together," I muttered.

"What was that?" Corrin asked, clearly picking up on my pettiness.

"Nothing, *Cor*," I said and edged toward the window to look out while my friend was clearly being chatted up by an alien.

I must have dozed off out of spite because the next thing I knew, Bailey was shaking me on the shoulder and the bus had stopped moving.

"We're here," he said.

As I stood to stretch, my leg cramped up a bit.

"You all go ahead. I'll catch up." I sat back down to work out a few of the kinks that had formed from sleeping with my head propped against a window and zero leg room.

"Okay, see ya in a minute," Bailey said, and they all exited the bus with the rest of the passengers.

I stood and was moving my legs around a bit to wake them when I looked up and glanced out the window. The Dora stood in the middle of a few dozen high schoolers, sorting through backpacks, tents, and sleeping bags, all of which had been haphazardly tossed into compartments underneath the bus when we left.

Then, I swear on everything Tolkien, it winked at me.

In an evil way.

I didn't realize winks could be evil, but there we were.

It was even more disconcerting because there wasn't even a glimpse of a smile involved. So, one of two things was happening: either it was evil, like I kept saying, or it was really, really, really bad at flirting. There was honestly no way to know for certain.

I wasn't even off the bus and was truly wondering why we had decided to come camping at all. Until I saw Bailey sling his gear bag across his back and click the straps on.

Bailey was good at a lot of things, but if you wanted to see him thrive, you asked him for advice on backpacking gear. He even had this really cool waterproof poncho thing you could inflate, and it made a cushiony bed that kept you both comfy and dry.

I was hoping he remembered to remove some of the things he usually had ready to go though, like the hatchet, and—

Oh, nope. He'd brought the hatchet.

He pulled it out just as a teacher reached over and took it from him. I was getting off the bus, and I heard him say, "Fine, but if we freeze because of lack of firewood, the fallout from us all getting frostbite is on you."

After setting up camp and getting the fire pits going, the teachers gave us several options, and Bailey, Corrin, and I went on the short hike, rather than do a ropes course or go swimming.

The hike was pleasant and blessedly accessible. We walked at a leisurely pace in a loop, up a small incline to a little lookout. The lakes in Oklahoma are massive and sprawling, so the view was expansive. We could hear other students splashing and jumping off a pier.

I wasn't quite ready to go diving off anything just yet, and there were way less of us on this climb, which made me happy too.

"You're being sorta quiet," Corrin said, walking alongside me on a wider part of the path. Bailey was out ahead, using both of his hiking sticks. He'd offered one to me, but this path was well kept so my cane was sufficient.

"Just wondering if anyone would notice if we went missing," I said.

"Whoa," she said. "That's grim."

"What? No, I just mean in like a 'let's ditch' kinda way." I laughed. "Like, would a teacher notice this second?"

She laughed. "Okay, but you do seem more contemplative than usual."

"It's all the Octavia Butler you're making me read."

"Well, either way, I think they'd notice and Bailey would murder you."

"Why me? Why not you?"

"Because he'd know I only left the party to keep you out of trouble."

"Fair enough."

We kept walking until we caught up to the group and Bailey. The teacher sponsor had brought a backpack full of snacks, so they passed around apples and sun-nut butter to munch on. Except for Bailey, who had brought his own protein liquid travel stuff and Monica Rogers who was allergic to both. Wooden benches lined the edge of the lookout so we all took seats to enjoy a quick rest, even though the walk wasn't particularly strenuous. It was a little chilly, but every few minutes people in boats on the water one would glide past and we'd all holler at it until they honked their horns.

Before too long, we were heading back though, because the teacher was clearly concerned we'd get lost in the woods.

We got back to the campsite, and the teachers had us help make food, which was just some MREs—meals ready to eat, aka, pouches full of freeze-dried food sludge that we added boiling water to. They were hit or miss, tastiness-wise. So, most of us passed around the different flavors, and everyone got a sample of the varieties.

Thankfully, someone's parents had packed them a cooler full of sandwiches from Big Al's Sub Shop, so we passed those around next and got full enough.

By then, it was getting close to dark, and there were five or six fires going. The teachers were paying less attention than they had been at the beginning of the night, and most of them were gathered around the same fire with a few of the nerdier nerds. Hail the high school hierarchy.

So, the evening, while totally supervised, still felt like a night in the woods with my friends.

We were just breaking out the s'mores when all of a sudden—I swear it was all of a sudden—the Dora was sitting right next to me on the log where I was balancing a chocolate bar and my newly toasted marshmallow. Like thigh-to-thigh next to me.

I shrieked and scooted over a good couple of inches, knocking into Bailey who yelped "Hey!" and barely saved his open pack of graham crackers from landing in the dirt.

"What do you want?" I said, a few notches louder than I probably should have.

"Hello to you too, silly," the Dora said.

Look, have you ever been called "silly" by one of your peers? It's not cute. Silly is a word that you reserve for addressing toddlers when you want to say something is stupid but you're not sure how the kid's parents will feel about you using the word stupid.

"What do you want?" I asked, this time in a relatively normal tone, but I was sure it came out sounding rather harsh.

"Just seeing what you all were up to," the Dora said, unblinking as usual, and its skin in the firelight had an unnatural glow to it. That slight shimmer just beneath the surface.

"Why are you being so weird, Chuck?" Bailey asked.

I tried to give him a shut-the-hell-up look, but it clearly didn't get through because he just kept munching on his s'more. "I'm not."

"I think it's cute." The Dora tilted its head about twenty degrees further than most people would. The gesture made its *Buffy Summers trying out for cheerleader* ponytail almost touch the ground. Okay, it was like a good three feet off the ground, but *still*.

"I'm not...cute," I said. Because of words. I was good at words.

"So, Chuck, will you come with me to the bathroom?" it asked because what even was my life?

"I don't really need to go, thanks."

It smiled at me in that half-smirk way I hate.

"I just need company. So many spooky things in the woods."

Bailey and Corrin were looking at me like I should obviously go, and I just... I hated everything because why couldn't they understand how horribly I wanted to not be going anywhere with this being.

And yet somehow, there I was, walking with it to the small structure with the campsite bathrooms. We got inside the wooden, fake log cabin-looking building and I truly did not have to go, so I decided it was a good time to wash my hands and fuss with my unruly hair.

The toilet flushed, and it came out and washed its own hands, staring at me in the mirror the entire time.

"I think we should go to the winter dance together. Wouldn't that be so silly?" it said out of nowhere.

I squinted at it. "Come again?"

"You and me," it said, smiling without showing a mouth full of perfectly straight white teeth. "We could go to the winter formal together."

"That's like two months away," I responded, as if that was an adequate follow-up to this alien flat out asking me on a date.

"Sure, gives us time to coordinate our formal wear."

"Our formal wear?" Now I *knew* it was an alien.

"I just want to get closer to you, Chuck. That's all." The Dora put a hand on my arm.

"Sorry, but I'm going to have to pass. Thanks, though?" In the smoothest way I could muster, I shrugged away from its touch. I opened up the bathroom door and headed back to the fire. I needed to get back to my friends and maybe see if there was enough reception out here to call a ride share.

Bailey and Corrin were sitting on the ground in front of a log together, eating the last bits of a chocolate bar, and I didn't even hesitate to sit smack dab between the two.

"Whoa, look out." Corrin moved her and Bailey's snack pile out of the way just as I plopped down.

"Y'all promise me you'll stay away from the Dora." I physically shuddered.

"What's this about?" Corrin took a bite of her s'more. "Did something just happen?"

"Yes," I said, looking at them gravely. "The Dora asked me on a date."

Was there a flash of something in Corrin's eyes?

All I got from Bailey was, "And that's why we need to stay away from her?"

"No, not that specifically," I said, "though now that I think about it, it is weird that the Dora is targeting me, given all the stuff with you-know-who."

"You're being paranoid," Corrin said.

"Look, I'm just trusting my gut, and my gut says no bueno."

"Fine," Bailey said. "We'll proceed with caution."

"Well, that is as noncommittal as just about anything you've ever said to me, Bailey Carter, but I'll accept it for now." I pulled my purple sleeping bag from our pile next to the log and laid it out between them. "Oh, and I'm freaking out so I'm going to need to sleep between the two of you so that whatever alien abduction happens, I get to have optimal protection."

"Wait, so you're—what? Sacrificing us?" Corrin said in mock disbelief.

"No, I'm saying you're *saving* me. Big, big difference," I assured her. "Now please tell me one of you squirreled away some extra graham crackers."

"Obviously." Bailey pulled out a full sleeve.

"This is why y'all are my best friends," I said.

Sleeping on the ground isn't the most comfortable thing. Luckily, between the warm fire at our feet and the various pads and bags Bailey had given us to cushion our backs against the dirt, I slept fairly well, and was not even more sore than usual when I woke up.

I'd drifted off to sleep, facing Corrin, the two of us whispering about nothing important, until long after the faculty sponsors had given up trying to make everyone sleep. Now, as they went around waking us up, I was glad it was not yet dawn so I could check myself for drool.

The three of us, along with the rest of the participating senior class members, climbed up to the cliff area to watch the sun rise.

Corrin had brought her gigantic fleece blanket and threw it around me, Bailey, and herself. I rested my head on her shoulder as we watched the sky turn from dark blue to pink to orange and red then back to blue but pale and soft.

It was nearly a perfect moment, but then I noticed the Dora standing perfectly still off to the side.

Facing away from the horizon and staring directly at us.

Before I could nudge Bailey or Corrin to look, the Dora had turned back toward the rising sun like the rest of us.

Chapter 12

After therapy a few days later, my mom pulled up to Bailey's, and I hopped out. We had the usual plans to stare at that dang cube and fuss about uncrackable codes, and we were hoping to do some character builds in case we ever got around to playing an RPG again.

His sister was standing in the middle of the front lawn when I walked up.

"Hi, Linda, what's up?" I asked.

She turned and looked at me slowly.

"Hello, Chuck," she drew my name out.

This kid was so odd, all the time. She was five years younger than Bailey, and we'd sometimes had to play with her, though lately she'd wanted nothing to do with us.

"You okay? You're being weirder than usual." I walked up to her and patted her on the head. "Did your Disney Channel subscription expire?" And usually, she would beam and laugh and act super offended when I gave her a mild ribbing.

But this time, she just blinked at me.

"Yes. My Disney subscription expired," she said, like she was puzzling out the words as she spoke them. I really wasn't sure what she was doing, but that was kind of par for the course with Linda.

"Right," I said, ambling toward the house, trying to figure out what in the heck was going on with her. "Well, I'm going to go head to the basement now."

"The basement is...empty," she said.

And finally, my mind began to wake up, and maybe what was happening was actually suspicious. Was this an alien thing?

"What do you mean, empty?" Panic built in my chest.

She didn't answer, and I rushed the rest of the way across the lawn and into the house.

I pushed my way through the crowded kitchen, shouting a quick greeting to Bailey's folks. They were always baking something, and on my way down into the basement, his dad offered me a literal loaf of bread to take home to my family. I had no idea where to put it and was in a rush to check on Bailey, so I just stuck it in my bag. That seemed like an okay choice to make. I was very good at choices.

I flung open the basement door and took the stairs as quickly as I could while maintaining relative safety.

"Bailey! Bailey!" I shouted as I rushed down.

The lights in the basement were dim as usual, and I heard no answer as I looked around frantically. "Bailey!" I shouted again, the fear bubbling in my throat.

"Chuck?" said a voice behind me, and I shrieked and jumped.

"Whoa, hey, it's me," Bailey said from the foot of the stairs.

"Where were you?" I flung myself at him and wrapped him in a hug that almost knocked us both down.

"Whoa, whoa," he said, hugging me back. "It's okay. I'm right here."

94

"Where did you go?" I asked, trying to calm my breathing.

"To the bathroom. You know, the one with the toilet upstairs?" He pulled back and studied my face. "Are you okay? Come sit down."

"Yeah, yeah, I'm okay." I took a seat at the D&D table, hoping the feeling would come back to my hands and feet soon. I was not good in a crisis. Was there a way to work on that?

"What happened?" He handed me a bottle of water and a plate of cookies. Like I said, they were constantly baking.

"Your sister said something really weird about the basement." I took a sip from the bottle, the panic receding.

"Linda?"

"Yeah."

"She is so freaking weird. Sorry about that."

"It was like really uncanny. She was acting really strange."

"Hold on." He walked to the foot of the stairs and hollered up to them. "Hey, send Linda down here, please!"

A few minutes later, she poked her head down. "What?" she asked, clearly annoyed.

"What did you do to Chuck?" he demanded.

She just shrugged, and I really had no idea how anyone dealt with twelve-year-olds.

"Did you change clothes just now?" I asked.

She looked at me like I was a complete moron. Then she just gave us both an enormous eye roll and disappeared back into the kitchen's fray, closing the basement door behind her.

"I think that was a panic attack," I said.

"Do you need me to call your folks?" he asked, concern in his eyes.

"No, I'll be okay, and we should try to get some of those characters built." I wanted to be someone who didn't panic just because a preteen was acting like a weirdo, but here we were.

"Okay, just let me know," he said, and started pulling out all the papers, maps, and dice we needed for the afternoon.

I wished I could have shaken the uneasy feeling I'd had, but I was pretty sure that was just my baseline now.

A few days later, we were back downstairs.

"I have a few more ideas." I dropped a brown file box full of notebooks onto the gaming table.

Bailey groaned and moved some of his D&D maps out of the way as I began unpacking it, clearly annoyed with me. "I thought we were going to start the campaign today?"

I glanced at his pile and saw a stack of character sheets and his lucky character roll dice. "Sure, sure, we can, but let's flip through these first. It'll only take a few minutes."

"What are they?" Corrin looked at the mismatch of spiral notebooks, several binders, a Trapper Keeper, and a stack of black-and-white composition notebooks.

"Listen, just don't judge me too harshly," I said. "I wasn't always the cool, suave creature you see in front of you."

Corrin let out a sharp laugh and grabbed the top notebook in the pile.

"'Mmm Bop and the Spring Fling,'" she read aloud from the front. I snatched it away, leaping halfway across the table as I did.

"Nope, that won't be any help." And I threw the notebook on the ground behind me.

"That was Hanson fanfic, wasn't it?" She gave me a dramatically disappointed look.

I sometimes worried that eventually no one would find me tolerable.

"No comment." I knew I was turning bright red even in the dim lights of the basement. "The others are sci-fi though, and lots of them have codes Pacey and Ghost and I used. I was thinking we could thumb through them and find something useful."

"Not a bad idea," said Corrin. "I just wish we knew what Pacey was trying to tell us. Might be easier to figure out how to figure it out."

Bailey sighed, picked up a different notebook, and flipped through the pages.

"I'll start with Roswell and Star Trek. You and Bailey can start with the later, more sophisticated stuff."

The next few minutes we spent combing through and comparing any made-up languages or ones based on fandoms to the notes Pacey had left but without any luck.

"Wow, you were *really* into Jean Grey." Corrin smirked at me.

"I swear if you read that out loud, I will never talk to you again." I snatched the X-Men-focused notebook from her.

"How did you *not* know you were queer back then?" She chuckled. "You barely even mention Wolverine."

"Some of us are late bloomers." I added the notebook to the stack of other ones that weren't helpful.

When we'd gotten through that stack, I ran upstairs to use the restroom and texted my folks that Bailey's folks had invited us to stay for dinner. As I walked back down the stairs, Bailey and Corrin were talking in hushed tones. I didn't overhear purposefully, but sometimes my ears did their own thing.

Corrin's voice rose from the bottom of the stairs. "I promise we'll start the campaign soon, Bailey. She just has to get this out of her system."

"Well, it's taking way too long," he said.

My shoes scraped the stairs loud enough for them both to look up.

"What's taking way too long?" I asked. My face had gone hot, and I knew they'd been talking about me.

"Just all this." He gestured toward all of the papers and notebooks and the cube and notes and the white board spread across the basement where we usually would have had campaign notes and art and whatever other projects we were working on.

"It's going to take as long as it takes." I squinted at him, not understanding what he was getting at. Or at least not wanting to.

"You just don't want them to be gone," Bailey practically shouted at me.

His vehemence took me by surprise. Bailey never got loud about anything.

"Chill out, B," Corrin said.

"No. No, I'm not going to 'chill out.'" He put air quotes around the chill out part, so we would know he meant it.

"What's your problem?" I asked, wishing immediately I'd chosen a slightly nicer phrase and tone, but seriously, what was his problem?

"You," he said, pointing at me, "are convinced that Ghost is alive. That there are *aliens* that took him. Don't you hear how totally unhinged that sounds? And you," he said, turning and pointing at Corrin. "You encourage her. You let it seem like nothing is weird about looking for secret alien codes everywhere."

"It's not just alien codes everywhere! It's literally alien codes on a specific page, right there." I was shouting a bit too now, and I wished I wasn't feeling so upset. "And it's not just me. Pacey obviously has some legit involvement too. Or did you forget they're on the run searching for Ghost."

"Hey, I'm just here to hang out and offer support to everyone." Corrin held her hands up.

"That's just as bad," he said. "You're encouraging her to keep looking for nothing. There isn't anything for us to find!"

"So then, how do you explain the Pacey stuff? And Ghost missing?" Then I registered what Corrin had added, and that bothered me too. "You're just here to offer support?" I asked, confused. "I'm confused."

In case you hadn't figured it out yet, my brain and mouth are connected in a direct line.

"Of course, I'm here to support you, Chuck." She looked at me the same way Bailey was, like I was totally out of the loop.

"You don't think anything is going on? You don't believe me? Or Pacey?" I felt like I was about to cry, and that sting in my eyes was really starting to piss me off, which was making me want to cry.

"I mean, I want to believe you," she started and reached a hand toward me, but I shrugged it off.

"But you don't?" I asked her pleadingly.

I needed her to believe me. I needed to not be the only one who knew something strange and otherworldly had happened.

Pacey had bailed on us, and I knew we had to figure this out. And now I was about to lose two-thirds of the planetary beings I could count on to help me sort through all of whatever this was.

"I'm not sure what I believe." She stepped toward me. "I know something is going on and that you and Pacey truly believe in this quest, but I am just not sure what is going to come of any of it."

"I gotta go," I said, and before either of them could say anything else, I did the mature thing and left.

I was outside, climbing onto my bike when Corrin came out behind me.

"Chuck, wait," she said.

"I just need a minute alone." I held my cane across the bars and got on. "But I'll see you soon."

Chapter 13

I wasn't sure where I was headed but wound up in the nature park where our abandoned oil drum was, just in time before the rain started. It was one of those cold late fall rains too, and just my luck it would end up being a full-blown storm.

I walked my bike the rest of the way to the silo and decided I had exercised enough for the day, so I sat on one of the wooden benches we'd made. I shot my folks a quick text so they wouldn't worry and let them know I'd be home later.

Everything was a mess.

Pacey was adventuring. Ghost was missing. Bailey was mad at me for essentially no reason I could figure out. And who knew what was going on with me and Corrin.

I closed my eyes and listened to the steadily increasing rain through the canopy of trees and onto the metal roof. The plop of the leaks in the ceiling onto the shallow puddles in the floor was familiar, but I was used to them being the background noise in a din of chatter with my friends.

I wanted to talk to Ghost.

Not only that, but I wanted to be with him wherever he was.

Not stuck here on Earth, where everything was boring and hard. I could picture him out there somewhere in space. Not doing homework. Ghost was always the sharpest of all of us, even if he really hated school. He could have graduated early, but he said he didn't want to miss out on all the fun of senior year.

He was definitely missing out on that, but I really hoped he was out there doing things way more exciting than school-sponsored sunrise sleepovers and no one believing anything he said, like me.

I must have dozed off but startled awake at the clap of thunder and a dark silhouette of a person holding back the plastic tarp covering the entrance on one side of the shelter.

"Ah, I don't have any money!" I shrieked and threw the closest thing I could find, which happened to be a granola bar, at the figure.

"For goodness sake, Chuck, chill out." Corrin stepped in the rest of the way, letting the blue tarp close behind her. She rubbed her arm where the granola bar weapon had whacked her.

"Oh, sorry, could I have that?" I was starving suddenly, and my body ached from accidentally napping on the wooden bench.

"Um, sure." She tossed it back at me and shook out her coat. Her hair was wrapped tight in a scarf, and she was wearing shorts and sneakers under her poncho. She sat next to me on the bench. "Lose track of time?"

"I guess I fell asleep." I offered her half of the granola bar.

She waved it away. "Well, text next time."

"What? I did!" I took out my phone and realized the text to my folks was still a draft and I had several in a row from them. "Oh, oops."

"Your folks sent me," Corrin said.

I groaned. "I'm so sorry, Corrin. It was an accident."

"I know it was, and I really don't mind. Your folks are just way more worried nowadays because of everything."

"Proof of life selfie?"

Corrin laughed. "Sure."

She leaned in next to me, and I hadn't realized I'd felt chilled until she pressed her warm arm against mine. She laid her head on my shoulder and flashed a peace sign while I took a quick picture.

"Let me see it first," she said, and I tilted my phone toward her so she could approve it. "Hey, we look cute! Send it to me too."

I took it back and was glad it was relatively dark in the shelter because I knew I was blushing. I shot off a text with the pic to my folks and made sure it sent and went from delivered to read.

They replied almost immediately with a thumbs-up emoji. Followed by "be home before 10."

I glanced at my clock. It was only just after seven, but the storm made it feel much later. The sky had to be solid clouds. There was a rumble of thunder in the distance, and the sound of the rain was steady and heavy. I turned off my screen and tucked my phone in my pocket.

"Did you walk here?" I asked.

"Yeah, I needed to clear my head anyway. Bailey and I talked for a while after you left."

"What about?"

"Mostly you."

"Oh. Um, okay."

She nudged my knee with hers. "Relax. Bailey is going to come around, and in the meantime, you and I can bust this mystery wide open if you want to."

"Maybe we shouldn't," I said.

"No way, Chuck. Don't even act like you're going to give up. If you think Ghost went to another planet and Pacey followed him there, you think I'm going to sit around and not figure out how to get there with you?"

"Okay, but what if it's like a really dangerous planet? What are the chances they're all friendly aliens?"

"Then we're just going to be smarter than they are."

"I still think the Dora is an alien."

"If I didn't know any better, I'd say you were jealous of her."

"Well, maybe I am. I don't know." I stood up and stretched my legs and shoulders since there wasn't room to pace, and I wasn't ready to head out yet.

Corrin stood up and looked at me. "Chuck. There isn't anything to be jealous of, and besides, *you're* the one she asked out, remember?"

She said it in that you're-being-totally-dense type of way she was fond of.

"Do you really need everything spelled out for you?" she asked softly and took a step toward me.

The sound of the rain disappeared. I might have stopped breathing.

"I mean, yeah, that would probably help." And then my body, which had a will of its own, took a step closer to her.

The sound of the wind stopped. My heart pounded in my ears.

We were almost toe to toe. She tilted her round chin up at me. I thought about touching it. And her lips parted just slightly.

"There you both are." Bailey burst in.

And I jumped so hard I hit my head on the metal roof and somehow clipped Corrin in the chin with my shoulder, and I was going to literally murder Bailey.

"It's storming so bad out there. We should probably get to an actual house." He was decked out to the nines in his best rain gear and tossed me a waterproof jacket.

"Oh, yeah, your folks sent Bailey out too," Corrin said, rubbing her chin.

Did she sound relieved? I didn't know. How did people ever figure anything out ever?

"I let them know she's safe and sound." She leaned up and gave me a gentle kiss on the cheek.

"Here, put these on too." Bailey handed me rain boots.

"Why do you have a pair of rain boots in my size, Bailey?" I asked.

"Always be prepared, duh." He shrugged.

"You're so strange." I tugged on the shoes. "This is strange, right?"

"I mean, yeah, but I'd expect nothing less from our Bailey." Corrin kissed him on the cheek too. "Let's all get home before they send out a third search party."

I wasn't sure who they would send, but I still felt extremely lucky that there were two proactive weirdos willing to tromp through the soggy woods to find me.

Corrin stepped out into the rain.

But before we left, I turned to Bailey. "Are we cool?"

"We'll be fine." He clapped a hand on my shoulder.

"Psst," I whispered.

"What now?" Corrin asked under her breath without turning around.

We were in class, and she literally had never been in trouble with a teacher.

"I just really like your hoodie." I might not survive this week. I could hear her eyes rolling again.

"Thanks, Chuck."

"You smell nice." This part I mumbled.

"What?"

"What?" I said way louder than a whisper. This finally got a glare from the substitute, clearly annoyed at having to look up from his crossword puzzle.

"Chuck, we have like six minutes left in class. Do you think you can try to maintain for that long?" Corrin asked in a text a few seconds later.

I couldn't help the flutter my stomach took when I noticed she'd changed her wallpaper to that pic of us from the other night.

I sent back a hang-in-there-cat meme and laid my head down on my desk.

I was always worried about time and running out and how long would things take my whole life. This situation was *not* making that part of my brain slow down.

After class, Bailey was running late, and I bounced on the balls of my feet while we waited for him.

"Chuck, you know I love you," Corrin said, "but did you remember to take your meds today?"

"Who needs meds?" I said in mock offense. "But also, I'll check."

While we waited for Bailey, I pulled out my Baby Yoda medicine bag. "See? Took my meds, I did."

"Just double checking."

"Thanks. Did you drink water?" I knew the answer was probably no and handed her my emotional support water bottle.

"I'm pretty sure we'd fall apart without one another." She handed the teal bottle back to me half emptied. When she did, our fingers brushed, and—I swear I'm not being dramatic—there was a spark.

"Ow!" She yanked her hand back. "You gotta stop shuffling your feet. That static electricity is ridiculous."

"Hey! The shuffling isn't exactly a choice." I shook my cane at her.

"Whatever, lady." She batted it away.

"Do you think he's going to show up?" I peered around the quad, looking for any sign of him. It felt like, for the second time in as many days, everything was unraveling. I could practically feel Bailey pulling away from us. At least in the ways that it mattered.

"He'd let us know if he was flaking," she said with more confidence than I was feeling.

This was turning out to be one helluva senior year. I couldn't wait to see what people we going to write in my yearbook.

Sorry, your friends all left one way or another. H.A.G.S.

Wish I'd gotten a chance to know you better, but you always seemed fine eating all alone forever.

Keep in touch, Cindy.

Why in my head I'm assuming I've asked people who do not know my name to sign my yearbook was just going to have to be left a mystery.

"So, are you planning on going to winter formal?" Corrin asked.

"What?" The question took me off guard for about seventeen reasons.

"Winter formal? Big fancy senior year dance? Happens during the winter?"

"Yeah, I know what the winter formal is. I just hadn't thought about it, I guess?" I said, unsure what was happening.

Was she asking me out?

What? No, that was probably definitely not what was happening.

"Well, I think we should go," Corrin said.

And I performed some sort of awkward, noncommittal shrug-nod movement with my head that I'm fairly certain has never been done before in the history of bodily movements.

When I said nothing, she started ticking off reasons on her fingers, as if explaining to her toddler sister. "Because it's fun. Because we need a break. Because it's been ages since I dressed up for anything. Because you would look cute dressed up. Because Ghost would have dragged us to it. For like a million reasons, Chuck."

"You think I'd look cute dressed up?" Then I gasped and held my hand to my chest as though utterly taken aback, to make sure if it wasn't a sincere comment, I could cover it up with that smooth, smooth sarcasm.

"I mean, you clean up fine when you try." Then she reached her soft brown hand up and brushed some of the curly hair out of my face. "Just need a little product to combat this frizz and you'd be ready to go."

"I'll be your girl," I said breathlessly. "Date. *Friend date.* We can go. We're friends."

I could hear the inward sigh as she dealt with my word vomit. It would be fine to run away, right? Like I knew she was my ride home and my best friend, but she wouldn't be too pressed, would she?

"Okay, we'll go to the dance together, then," she said as if it was the most settled thing in the world.

Before I had a chance to say anything else ridiculous enough to make her change her mind, Bailey finally showed up, and we buckled up into Corrin's car.

"How about, instead of doing alien stuff this afternoon, we just play a board game?" I said, surprising even myself.

"Really?" Bailey asked, excited.

"That sounds good to me." Corrin beamed. "Want me to swing by Sonic on the way?"

I wanted to be happy with my friends and do things that made them happy, even if there was a constant tug in the back of my head to keep searching.

"Sure, my treat."

Chapter 14

The night of the art show I asked my mom for a ride since I was already running late. She said sure, which gave me time to put a few moments of consideration into what I was wearing. I opted for a button-up mushroom-print shirt and black slacks, rather than my usual worn blue jeans. Super artsy of me. I smudged on a bit of eyeliner and ran my fingers through the less mangled curls.

I was, frankly, dreading this. I knew the Dora was going to be around, and I just didn't want to with that whole situation.

But I had promised Corrin.

Corrin was standing at the entrance of the art gallery when we got there. The door was propped open to the crisp fall air, and she was greeting people as they walked in. She wore a black blazer and blue sequin shorts with black boots. She had slicked her hair back on the sides, and the top was a beautiful series of braids and poofs. Her makeup was flawless. Understated and meticulous.

Turned out Corrin had been way more interested in doing art curation and hosting shows than I had known. Even my mom noticed.

"Wow, Corrin looks so professional!" she said as she pulled up to the curb to drop me off.

I looked down at my own outfit and audibly gulped.

My mom chuckled. "You look fine for an art show on a weeknight in Tulsa."

"Thanks for reminding me of the high standards you hold me to, Mom," I said sarcastically. I leaned over and gave her a quick hug.

"Call us if you need a ride, and don't be out too late."

"Will do. Thanks, Mom." I climbed out, shutting the door behind me. I waved goodbye, but when I turned around, the Dora was there, standing elbow to elbow with Corrin.

It looked up at me as I approached and threw its head back in laughter at something Corrin had said, resting a hand on her elbow. "Oh my gawd, Corrin, you crack me up. You're so clever."

Corrin beamed at it, and my eyes narrowed. I cleared my throat.

"Hi, Corrin." I nodded curtly at the Dora. "Dora."

"Oh hiiii, Chuck," the Dora said.

"Thanks so much for coming!" Corrin said. "I have to get inside to keep circulating, but I'll be back soon, promise."

"I better go too and check on my art. Fingers crossed I sell something tonight," the Dora said, grinning but showing no teeth. It was like it had half a dozen totally different smiles. It wore a dress that made it look like it belonged on the set of *Little House on the Prairie*. Its blonde hair was braided in a crown around its head. I was pretty sure it didn't have on any makeup, but its skin looked flawless too. I hated it.

But not because I was one of those women who liked to shame other people for being pretty or anything. I was just fairly certain it was pure evil.

"Cool," I said under my breath. "I was really hoping to be on my own at this thing."

I texted Bailey, but he said he wasn't going to make it. I considered not even going inside and just walking to the coffee shop, but this was important to Corrin and it was probably best we didn't get left alone with the Dora.

So, in I went.

The gallery was bigger than I expected. The owners of the art supply shop where Corrin worked had repurposed a three-car garage shop across from their store. They'd taken out all the car repair things, of course, but left the metal ceiling and the giant lifts that were mounted throughout. The floor was cement, and it looked like they could still operate the big doors if they wanted to. Otherwise, it looked about what I expected of an art gallery. Lots of art on all the walls a huge spread of snack foods, and a place to get drinks in the corner.

I moseyed over in the general direction of cheese and crackers and took in some of the artwork as I passed, but mostly I was just wondering what types of cheese and crackers there would be.

The coolest thing was a gigantic octopus made entirely out of textiles. See, I knew big words. Its design was simple. Just two colors of fabric, gray on the top and off-white on the underside, plus big, poofy, white eyes. The fabrics were textured slightly, and the artist had rested the soft sculpture across a large block, so its tentacles hung off each side.

I wanted to use it as my forever reading place, and also, it was just a tiny bit creepy. I walked closer to get a better look. It was at least twice as long as I was. I imagined the artist might have had to strap it to the roof of their car to get it anywhere. Then I imagined the artist dragging it with them on a bus, and it made me laugh out loud.

"Do you like it?" the Dora asked.

"Ack!" I squealed. How did it always manage to sneak up on me? This was such a huge open space. How?

"I asked if you like it, silly," it said, staring at me unblinkingly. I considered offering it some eye drops.

"Um, yeah, it's pretty cool."

"I think so too," it said, holding a cup of what I'm pretty sure was wine and looking at the sculpture.

Was this what I was expected to be doing at an art show? Just standing around, looking at the art, and telling other people I thought it was cool? What did I do if I thought it wasn't cool? What if I accidentally told whoever the artist was that I didn't like a piece, and it was theirs?

I decided I might just have to keep my mouth shut the entire night.

Art shows were stressful.

I must have been standing there frozen and unspeaking for long enough to make it weird. Because the Dora eventually walked away.

I shifted my focus. Cheese. Cheese and crackers.

Something to chew so I didn't have to talk my way out of a minefield of my own creation.

I thought Corrin must have sensed my growing unease because, before I knew it, she was walking over to me with a bottle of water.

"Come on, let me introduce you to some people." She walked me over to where a couple of older hippie folks were looking at a triptych panel depicting a bunch of dogs cheating while playing casino games. Which I supposed was a modern take on the dogs playing poker?

Turned out they were Corrin's bosses and spoke highly of her, so we got along just fine. But I was still pretty worn out from all the socializing.

To be honest, I was pretty much only sticking around for the gouda and to keep an eye on Corrin. The art was cool, but the people were giving me really intellectual-people vibes, in a tense way.

I was caught between really wanting to just go to bed and not wanting to risk leaving Corrin alone with the Dora, even though I couldn't imagine it trying something too shady in this crowd. I really didn't like the way the Dora kept touching Corrin's arm for no good reason.

I was hovering by the cheese table when I saw the Dora get a drink from the bar area and take it over to Corrin. It had such we're-on-a-date energy that I crushed the plate with my salami on it in my fist.

I'd made my appearance, and it was time to go. So, I texted my folks and gave Corrin a quick wave then made my way to a bench I'd seen outside.

Being the middle of fall in Oklahoma, it should have been cooler, but suddenly everything felt stifling even outdoors. I needed air, and the bench seemed like the best choice. I considered wandering over to the coffee shop but decided to just stay put.

While I was sulking, the front door of the gallery swung open, and when I glanced up, Corrin and the Dora both came out, holding the drinks the Dora had gotten for them. Right as they stepped outside, the lights strung all across the square and around all the buildings turned on. Corrin made a small happy sound.

It made me wish I had another plate of salami to crush.

"It's all a matter of timing." The Dora smiled up at her.

I cleared my throat. "I mean, it happens at the same time every day."

"Well, yeah, but it's fun to see them turn on." Corrin gave me a stop-being-weird look. "I'll see you tomorrow morning, Chuck."

She and the Dora went back inside to probably say important things about art through the ages and its impact on society as a whole. I crossed my arms, not wanting to admit why I was so terribly annoyed about whatever that was.

My mind wanted to focus on anything else, but of course, when I asked it to, it would never comply. I wished Ghost was here for me to run things by, but I just leaned my head back and waited for my parent to come pick me up.

Chapter 15

"So, any chance you need some money to buy a dress or suit?" my mom asked. I had made the fatal error of telling her that Corrin and I were maybe going on an actual date to an actual dance but that probably it was as friends, and I regret ever speaking to a single grownup ever in my life.

Technically, my mom was kinda cool, and I would admit that with the standard amount of begrudging teenage attitude. She knew I may want to wear a dress. Or a suit. *And* she knew I was broke and would probably wait until the last minute and end up stuck wearing something awful I found in the back of my closet.

Speaking of the back of my closet, I was standing in the middle of my room with practically every single piece of clothing I owned in piles all around me. Straight up Marie Kondo style but without the joy because nothing felt right.

"Need some donation bags?" she asked.

I looked around the room in a despair-adjacent way.

I was an impulse bargain clothes shopper and also have no control when it comes to saying no to people giving me free stuff. It's a combination of "I have to be polite" and also "I might wear that someday, who knows?"

Having several cousins in town who are older than me by a variety of years meant for my whole life my closet had been a revolving door of hand-me-downs and impulse purging when my ADHD and anxiety meshed and decided it was time to clear out physical clutter for an entire day.

"Yes, please," I said, realizing I'd already started sorting them into piles, not just for formal versus not formal.

She came back with a couple of laundry baskets and a few big black contractor garbage bags.

"Company?" I asked.

And she said, "Sure thing," and plopped onto my bed, where she started folding some clothes that were in the keep pile, without me even having to ask.

A few years ago, she and I had a long conversation about parents asking if their kids wanted company and kids feeling like they can't say no to that question. So, being the rad humans we are, we flipped it around, and now she knew that, if I wanted company, I'd ask. It started out as a joke, but I was really glad because before I'd always felt weird. Like I was being too needy. Or acting like a little kid.

Anyway, it was our system, and it worked for us and I was glad she stayed. I was also glad she didn't immediately start peppering me with questions. Even though I'm sure she had a few on her mind.

Which was probably why I opened my big mouth.

That woman can play me like a fiddle.

"I just don't know if she *like* likes me, you know?" I said.

"Corrin?" she asked, confirming before we kept going. She always liked to clarify things before continuing unless I was just on a ramble.

"Yeah. Corrin."

"Does she know how you feel?"

We both kept folding clothes, me haphazardly and tossing every other item into the giveaway bag, her with precision she knew full well would get tousled four minutes after I decided to roll out of bed the next morning.

"Even I don't totally know how I feel." I flopped dramatically onto the bed.

She ran her fingers through my hair like when I was a little kid and having trouble at school or with a friend or just for the sake of being mopey.

"Someone else asked me out too," I said, not quite sure why I brought it up. But the whole encounter with the Dora had been so unsettling.

"Oh really? Anyone I know?"

"I don't think so," I said, then went on. "We met at the paint shop and have seen each other around at school stuff lately."

"Do they have a name?"

"The Dora. Well… Dora. I say 'the Dora.'"

"Do you like this 'the Dora'?"

"No, I really don't. Not even as a friend." I paused to come up with a word that fit just how I felt about the Dora and coming up blank because *I'm pretty sure it's my mortal enemy* might sound a tad overly dramatic, even for me.

We folded clothes quietly for a few more minutes.

"I just thought I'd tell you," I said. "I know I've been distracted lately." She let out a gentle laugh.

"More than usual, I mean."

"We noticed. But I don't think you really need to focus that much to figure out how you feel about Corrin."

"She's my best friend, Mom. What if I really mess it up?"

"That could happen—" she began.

I interrupted her with a groan. "Hey, thanks for the pep talk."

"Let me finish," she continued. "But it may not. And just about the only time I see you thrilled lately has been with Corrin. So, no matter how she feels about you or you feel about her, you should try to have fun at this dance."

I took a deep breath and nodded.

"I'm gonna need a suit."

We went shopping the next day, and I was so glad I had folks who gracefully weathered my ever-changing style vibes.

My mom helped me pick out a really snazzy suit. It fit surprisingly well without needing any sort of tailoring, and I even worked in time for a haircut with her.

Her exact words when I asked were, "Oh heavens, yes, please."

I laughed and shook my hair in front of my face. "You're not a fan of the emo shaggy dog look?"

So, it was a whole day, and it made me feel really glad to be doing something with my mom that focused on fun things and not just working on PT or counseling or reminding me about school stuff.

She even blessedly left me more or less alone about the date thing too, other than asking if Corrin was planning to match me and if I needed to coordinate my tie or vest or if we were going to wear corsages.

Eventually I just let her dictate questions to me so I could text them to Corrin, who almost immediately texted back asking if I was okay, so I had to reassure her that, yes, I was okay, just shopping with my mom.

Turned out she did like the idea of corsages and coordinating.

So, good call, Mom.

On the way home, we even stopped for ice cream, and it might have been in the top ten days I've had with my mom.

It felt so good to be pampered and chat about things that weren't a huge deal.

Except for the Corrin part. That part was huge.

But also, if I wanted anyone to know about my first proper date with someone I had my first proper feelings about, I was glad it was my mom. Though the sting of missing Ghost popped up more than once.

Plus, I looked like a freaking femme James Bond in my suit, and I would have worn it to school the next day if my mom hadn't told me that was a terrible idea. I begrudgingly agreed.

When she stepped out of the car to pick me up on the night of the dance, Corrin looked like the results of a Pinterest search for 'aesthetic dream.'

She had her hair in space buns that had tiny diamond pins in them and wore a dress with a sequin top that changed from silver to a black as she moved and a tulle skirt that was black and speckled with tiny silver beads that looked like stars twinkling in the night sky. Her dark brown skin glowed against the colors of the dress as she twirled around to show it off.

Corrin looked so soft and warm. It was like my body had a mind of its own, and I moved toward her and barely caught myself with my cane as I tripped over my feet because I was definitely not looking where I was going.

Her shoes were spiky heels that Bailey had painted to look like galaxies. I had a matching paint job on my Converse, but it looked much better on Corrin.

I was not cool. But I felt like if I was close enough to Corrin, her coolness might radiate onto me. She was picking me up for a dance, and all I could think was we were going to maybe dance together which meant I'd get to touch her. Shoulders? Hands?

I was losing it. Was I drooling?

"You look stunning, Corrin," my parent said and took a picture of her as she struck a pose.

"Get in there, Chuck," they said, and the two of us stood side by side.

Corrin grabbed me by the waist, laughing, and planted a kiss on my cheek as my parent snapped a thousand pictures. My mom was simultaneously giving instructions on turning it to portrait mode and trying to get us to keep still so they could figure it out.

"You're loving this, aren't you?" I said, my cheeks literally on fire.

"You have no idea," Corrin said, laughing, and she turned to straighten my tie. I went with a long, skinny, black, vintage one that belonged to one of my great grandpas. I always had good luck when I wore it.

"*Okay*, we have to go," I said, giggling at my parents.

"Can you please send me *all* those pictures?" Corrin asked as she dragged me away to her Honda. "Chuck will forget if I ask her to do it."

"Of course, dear, you both be safe," my mom said as we got in the car.

"Bye, girls, have fun!" my parent said as we buckled up and drove away.

Corrin turned on the stereo and cranked up The Smiths, so we both sang along as we headed to the dance.

"Aren't we picking up Bailey?" I asked as we turned left instead of right on his street.

"Nope, our sweet angel child Bailey got himself a date." Corrin beamed. "I helped him get ready and everything. He's wearing a tuxedo, Chuck! Bailey is in an honest-to-goodness tux."

"Really? How did I not know that?" I asked excitedly, "Who is it?"

"I'll tell you, but don't freak out."

"Why would I freak out?"

"Okay, well don't get weird about it."

"I'm almost never weird, Corrin."

"You will not believe it, but Dora! And *she* asked *him*!"

"Oh, really? That's…fine," I said.

"That's it? That's all you have to say?"

"Well, you're obviously expecting a reaction from me, so you know what I really think."

"I just don't understand why you are so down on Dora."

"I didn't say that…exactly."

"What are you saying then?" She let out a huff. I could tell this was one of those times in my life where I was about to hit a nerve head on and should just stop talking because anything I said was going to be wrong.

"I'll try to be excited for him, I guess. I didn't think he was even going." I tried to cover just how very unexcited I was.

I really didn't want to tell Corrin that the Dora gives me the full-blown heebie-jeebies again because I felt like a broken record about it. It was like any time I talked about the Dora, they just forgot everything I'd said.

"Well, yeah, he wasn't because he didn't want to be a third wheel," Corrin said, gripping the steering wheel.

"It's always the three of us though."

"Yeah, Chuck, that's the point." She sighed and turned up the music. "Let's just enjoy tonight."

I nodded. "Yeah, of course."

The school party planning committee—I assumed that was what it was called—had splurged on an actual venue, not just decorating the school cafeteria or gym with crepe paper. So, the drive was taking us a bit out of town, along the same road we took to the quarry.

I couldn't help but hope I could keep all the alien buzz out of my brain for the night, and I let myself look over at Corrin.

"What?" she said, glancing at me and grinning.

"Nothing, I'm just…"

Suddenly, Corrin screeched and slammed on the brakes.

"What the fuck!" I yelled. Then I saw them.

"Pacey?" Corrin yelled.

Pacey had run out directly in front of the car, and Corrin had barely stopped in time to keep from hitting them. Corrin unlocked the doors quickly, and they ran to the back seat, yanking it open.

"Drive," they said.

"What is going on?" Corrin yelled back at them.

"We have to motor. I'll explain on the way," they said.

"Well, buckle up," she said and took off. "Am I going anywhere in particular?"

"The quarry."

Corrin looked at me sideways, and I gave her a small shrug.

"I'm really not dressed for a swim," I said, trying, as usual, to lighten whatever mood this was with sarcasm.

"If my calculations are correct, we won't be swimming." Pacey shrugged their backpack and jacket off and buckled up. They rolled up their sleeve, and I noticed blood. A metric shit ton of blood.

"You're bleeding!" I said.

"You better not bleed on my car. My folks will kill me." Corrin fumbled in the center console for the pile of drive thru napkins that always collected there. She handed them back to Pacey, and they dabbed at the oozing cut.

"That looks bad! What happened?" I unbuckled and climbed into the back seat to help them.

"Watch the buns," Corrin said as I squeezed past her. Not sure if she was referring to my butt or her hair. I'd wager a guess it was the latter.

"Sorry," I said.

"And buckle up. don't make me say it again." Corrin is like really strict about safety.

"The go-bag is in there." Pacey nodded to their backpack, and I rummaged through it, pulling out the first aid kit.

"Should I pull over so we can switch places?" Corrin asked me.

"There isn't time, and Chuck will do fine. I'll talk her through it," Pacey said as though I wasn't there.

"Hey, I'm right here!" I said indignantly. Though if I'd had to choose any of us to have tasks during a first aid crisis, I would not have made the top of that list. Corrin and Pacey, on the other hand, had experience that I didn't.

And Bailey was so great at stuff like this because of all his Scout training.

And Ghost would know what to do.

"Chuck!" Pacey said firmly, and I snapped out of it. "I'm going to need you to stop Chucking so hard right now."

Corrin snorted and said, "Chucking" under her breath. Just what I wanted, my name to be a verb meaning ADHDing so hard you couldn't stop the blood gushing out of your best friend.

"You can do this," Pacey said, grabbing my elbow with their uninjured hand.

I nodded. "Okay."

"And Corrin," they said, looking up at her, "any chance you have that device with you?"

Chapter 16

Pacey was bleeding all over the upholstery, and it was my turn to do the *saving my best friend's life* thing. I quickly tossed some peroxide on the cut.

"Ow, Chuck, that fucking stings," they said.

"It's for the diseases." Then I wrapped up their arm tight with some gauze and a bandage. "Ta-da!"

"Did you seriously just 'ta-da' while patching my *gaping wound?*" Pacey practically screamed, exasperated.

"Just call me Doctor McDreamy."

"Give me strength," Corrin muttered under her breath. She was rifling in the glove box but still managing to keep the car steady.

"I've missed you both so much," Pacey said suddenly, exhaustion streaking their face.

"You gonna tell us what's going on, and where we're going?" Corrin asked.

"Keep driving but yes. Also—" Pacey turned and looked in the rearview mirror behind us. "Shit, we have company."

I couldn't help but grin. "You sound like such a badass. High five."

"Oh my god no, Chuck," Pacey said. "There is about to be a fight if we don't get to the quarry fast enough. Step on it, Corrin."

"Look, I'm driving as fast as I can."

I glanced at the speedometer. "You're going forty-five."

"Which is five miles *over* the speed limit," she said. "This is as fast as we go."

After tossing the owner's manual and the tire pressure gauge onto the floor, she popped open the hidden compartment in the glove box and handed the square device back to Pacey.

"I'm so freaking glad you have this," they said. Pacey rummaged in their coat pocket and produced a similar-looking device, but this one had definitely caught fire at some point. "Toss this out the window, hard, Chuck. It may slow them down a few minutes."

I did as they asked then turned back.

"Who is after you?" I asked, looking through the rear window. The road we were on was winding, and I saw little behind us, aside from the forest.

"It's not really a who but more like a what," Pacey said.

I rummaged around in the backpack for other doctor-y items that could be useful. "What do you mean, a 'what'?"

"They're not really a 'who' type of species. Turns out there are at least a couple types around, but these big sorta oaf blobs are really bad news. And they are NOT happy with me right now."

"What did you do?" I asked, my eyes wide and my mouth agape.

"Whoa, whoa, whoa, slow down. Are you *seriously* talking about aliens right now?" Corrin said from the front seat.

"Yes, and I know it's not really nice to refer to a group of sentient things as 'whats,'" Pacey said, "But y'all know I'm sensitive to that sort of thing, and that's just how it is with these blobs."

"Pacey, my issue was NOT with your speciesism or whatever, but I need you to clarify the 'aliens' bit," Corrin said, gripping the steering wheel even tighter.

"I fucking knew it," I said and threw my fist into the air triumphantly.

"*Breakfast Club?*" Pacey asked, smiling at me.

"You know it."

That was when the brakes on the car slammed down, and Pacey and I both lurched forward—not too far though because safety first, friends. Corrin screeched the car onto the shoulder and yanked on the emergency brake. She spun around, her space buns bobbing and her shimmering dress catching the light.

It was almost enchanting enough for me to miss the ire in her eyes, which I noticed she had detailed with perfect wing tips and purple eye shadow.

"What. Is. Going. On?" she demanded.

"Okay, sorry. I'll focus, but please drive," Pacey pleaded.

"And you?" Corrin looked at me, one eyebrow raised.

I closed my mouth and made a locking motion and threw away the key. She nodded, satisfied, and pulled onto the road, just as an orange Ford Pinto came into view.

"Punch it, Chewie," Pacey said and crouched down in the seat. "Please?"

"Start talking, Pacey," Corrin said.

"Aliens are real. Ghost pissed some off. He's very much involved in some interplanetary stuff. And he has got a couple of species riled up in a bad way."

"Told y'all he wasn't dead," I said smugly then locked my lips right back up after the rearview mirror look I got.

"There are several species that already have an established presence on Earth or within our solar system. But humans keep royally messing things up, and so most of the aliens keep waffling on if they actually want to ask us to join up with their alliances or just like let us alone to figure things out."

"Cool, that's just great to hear." Corrin's sarcasm was deep enough to cut through a Congressional hearing on climate change. "So, why are they after *you*?"

"I might have given away their Earth base location, and it might have sort of been targeted by some G-men. Aliens don't actively seek the Area 51 treatment," Pacey said. "And I may have kind of led them there."

"That sounds really bad," she said.

"You have no idea," Pacey confirmed. "And these dudes don't mess around."

"But you said there's more than one species?" I asked, excited.

"Yeah, I don't know about all of them, of course, but there are a few," Pacey said. "And Ghost is working with some who, as far as I can tell, actually don't want Earth to just like burn itself out. But that means he's the enemy of some who do."

"So, you *both* somehow have enemies from other planets?" I asked, simultaneously appalled and impressed. Not a single alien species wanted me dead at all yet.

Just then, Pacey looked me up and down and asked, "Wait. Where were you going?" They looked at Corrin and took in her outfit as well. "Were you on a date?"

"Stop squealing," I said. "It's just a school dance."

"Oh my gosh, I'm so sorry," they said.

"You were literally bleeding out and jumping into the road," I pointed out. "We can miss the dance."

"But was it a date?" they asked me a quietly, eyebrows raised.

I gave what was probably the most confused look of my life, along with a shrug. "Wait, if you didn't know we'd be driving to the dance, how did you find us?"

"Oh, I have a modified GPS type tracker on your car and on Chuck. Figured those would come in handy."

"What?" I asked and began patting myself down. "That is so cool, and also, I'm really mad and feel slightly Big Brothered."

"Okay, we're almost there. Can you please hurry up, and fill us in on what is going on with a little more detail?" Corrin was pushing fifty now.

"Yes, he's alive," Pacey said. "I don't know all of what happened, but he's on the run right now. I have some leads and a contact who should be able to help me find him."

"And these aliens are chasing you because you ratted them out to the feds, but they're different from the ones chasing Ghost." Corrin clarified.

"I mean, 'ratted out' is kinda harsh," Pacey hedged. "More like called in the feds as a diversion while I tried to steal one of their spaceships?"

"I knew I should have gone with you." I lamented my boring at home life trying and failing to solve alien writing puzzles and Rubik's Cubes.

"Point is," they said, "they're mad, and I have to try to make a portal jump at the right coordinates to meet up with my contact before they catch up to us. If I don't, they can take manual control over the portal, and then we're all screwed."

Corrin turned off onto the side road to get the car onto the access road that ran parallel to the train tracks and toward quarry.

"Okay, so to summarize," I said, "you need to jump through the portal, and you're running out of time, and it's to save Ghost and maybe Earth."

"Yes," Pacey said.

"And they're in that dorky little car back there?" Corrin asked, looking in the rearview mirror.

Pacey spun around. "Shit. Yup. Y'all listen when I say they are aliens, I mean *alien* aliens. Not like a little bit of face makeup and a wrinkly nose alien. But more like the Oogie Boogie guy from *Nightmare Before Christmas*. But with more ooze."

"Eww that sounds really awful." Corrin wrinkled up her nose.

"Yeah," Pacey agreed, "and they don't mind hitting things. And they're also pretty fast."

"So, anything we can do to stop them? Or slow them down?" I was really eager to get in on the action.

"Other than tossing out my portal remote in case that's what they were tracking, then no. Honestly, I haven't really had much time experimenting with fighting the giant killer alien blobs, Chuck, not to my knowledge. But I'll be sure and try some things out next time and add them to my list of alien notes for you."

"Look, I know we're all under a lot of stress, but I'm going to need you to clarify whether or not you're being sarcastic right now." I said.

"Chuck!" They both yelled at the same time.

"Ugh, fine, we're here anyway," I said and sure enough, we were approaching the train track bridge. But Corrin wasn't slowing down.

Chapter 17

"Corrin, slow down."

"We can make it," she said and, honest to Zeus, put on her sunglasses.

I wish I had had time to react, or take a picture or something, but before I could do a thing, we were driving on that old broken-down, rusty AF bridge we'd carefully walked across a thousand times.

And it was working.

Kind of.

To be perfectly honest, I had my eyes closed for most of the time, but based on Corrin's screaming and the rumbling crashing sounds behind us, we were definitely cutting it close.

Only when we screeched to a stop and I heard Pacey exclaim, "Holy balls, Corrin," did I open my eyes and see that we had indeed made it across what had been a bridge moments ago.

All three of us turned around and saw the tiny orange car stop at the edge where the bridge used to begin. Could you call something a bridge if its main function was to get something from one side to another and there was no way that was going to happen anymore?

The rails had almost completely collapsed, and the track was swinging below the level of the bridge edges. Technically, the track was still attached to itself, but the metal was swaying and making super creepy popping sounds that I did not want to think too much about.

It looked like any second now the whole mess would fully collapse in on itself.

The tiny car revved its engine from across the chasm and flashed its lights in a menacing way.

"Um, is that a spaceship?" I asked, wondering if there would be spacey engines coming out the back and if we would get to see it jump across the river.

"What? No, that's a Ford Pinto," Pacey said.

"Oh, like actually a Pinto? Not a souped-up alien one?"

"They probably would have caught us by now if that was the case, don't you think?" Pacey said as if that was the most obvious thing in the world.

"Is it safe to get out of the car?" Corrin asked.

"Yeah, we gotta hurry."

"Why can't we keep driving?" I asked then noticed the steam pouring out of the engine. "Oh."

The three of us scrambled out. It took a second to take in all the damage, but the poor little Honda Accord new Oklahoma driver starter pack was done for. All four of the tires were popped, and it was definitely bent in places where cars shouldn't be bent.

If we survived this, Corrin's parents were going to be livid.

"I drove over those rocks." Corrin grimaced and pointed to a few barrier boulders streaked with tan paint from her bumper. Which itself was about ten yards away and bent at a really horrible angle.

It was then that I looked over at the other side again and saw the aliens getting out of the car.

"Do you think they can get across?" I started to ask.

Then Corrin and I got our first really good look at these things.

Big. Bumpy. Old pickle colored.

When I say big, I mean massive. Clowns coming out of a clown car gargantuan, scale-wise. Each one—there were three—by the way, towered over the car and was wide from top to bottom.

They were a gross sewage color, like when your dog eats too much grass and pukes it up, then eats it, then pukes it up again. Bile and slimy and brown.

"I'm gonna be sick." Corrin turned away to get a breath. But the wind had shifted, and these things had a smell to match their good looks.

"Here." Pacey handed us both masks they'd grabbed from their backpack. "This will help a little."

"Where are their heads?" My brain was just not understanding what was happening with their bodies. It wanted to see arms, legs, heads, etc. But there were just ambulatory blobs, and they were, incidentally, beginning to amble our way. I pointed at the shredded bridge. "They can't get across that, can they?"

"No, they weigh like a thousand pounds each," Pacey said. "In space, it doesn't matter how much you weigh because of gravity stuff."

"But they can apparently climb," Corrin said. "They're going down." True fear caused a tremble in her voice, and sure enough, they were beginning to climb/slide/blob-roll down the side of the cliff toward the creek below.

"Um, we gotta go," I said, eyes wide, and started walking as fast as I could. Thank the maker I had been keeping up with my physical therapy. Okay "keeping up" might have been a bit of an exaggeration, but I did it sometimes. At least enough times to fill out my habit tracker to a reward level.

Pacey hadn't been lying when they said these things were legit threatening.

Corrin told me she'd be right behind me and ran to her trunk. When I glanced back to make sure she was coming, she had ripped off her sequined heels and quickly shoved on tennis shoes. Sigh, she was basically a superhero.

"What in the second Bush administration are those?" Corrin asked, eyes as wide as mine, and she was hurrying with me and Pacey now as we made our way to the quarry jump spot.

"That's not a phrase people use," I said as we pushed our way down the path. "Is it?"

"Not the point, Chuck."

"I told you, aliens. Bad aliens. Aliens we need to run from. Well, aliens *I* need to run from. Sorry to drag you all into this," Pacey said.

"Are you really, though?" I huffed.

"Well, okay no," they admitted. "I've missed y'all."

"You are both the worst," Corrin said. "There are literal blob monsters chasing us."

"Wild, isn't it?" Pacey said, grinning.

We made it to the quarry's edge in record time. And I was pretty pleased with myself that I wasn't more winded. But the self-congratulatory mood evaporated rapidly when we heard the creatures crashing through the forest. I was really hoping it would take them longer to get back up the cliff, but apparently, they had figured it out.

Too bad they weren't completely stupid blobs.

"What do we do?" Corrin asked.

"I have to get through the portal before they have time to lock me out." Pacey pulled out the cube, and with several deft clicks and turns, it beeped and the portal pulsed on, brighter and more visible than I'd ever seen it.

"Whoa, so that's what it does?" I asked.

"I mean, yes?" Pacey said.

Corrin groaned.

"The code was to help you figure out how to activate the portals," Pacey said. "Sort of like a subway map for this sector. Just gotta have it within range of the portal."

"So, it wouldn't work, in say, Bailey's basement?" I grimaced.

"What? No," Pacey said. "Did y'all not even think to come out here?"

Corrin groaned again, and the crashing grew louder.

"I think you two should hide," they said and started the timer on their old-school wristwatch, watching the portal as it began emitting a humming noise.

"No way, we're not hiding while you're in danger," she said. She'd grabbed her pocket mace from her purse and the tire iron from her trunk. She was so fierce, and I was literally in love.

"I'm going to be fine," Pacey said. "We just need to wait a few more seconds."

The crashing was getting closer, and I kid you not, a fucking deer family burst out of the woods and turned like inches before careening off the quarry edge. Birds were flying out of the trees, and I thought pretty much every squirrel had noped out of there too.

"They're getting too close. We can't outrun them," Corrin said.

She reached out for my hand, and I squeezed it in mine, hoping we were equally sweaty in like a cute, matching way.

"We have to jump with you!" I said just as the portal shimmered and then pulsed slightly brighter and changed into a different color.

"Then jump!" Pacey yelled.

As the three towering, smelling angry blobs burst out of the edge of the forest, several things happened almost simultaneously.

The three of us turned and ran the couple of steps needed to jump off the platform and into the portal.

My leg fell through one of the boards.

Corrin, still holding my hand, turned to pull my foot out.

Pacey yelled that we had to jump, now.

The monsters were closing the distance. I looked up at Corrin, in the sunset, her shiny galaxy dress glittering.

And I pushed her back as hard as I could.

"No!" she yelled as the portal swallowed her and Pacey up.

I turned around to face the baddies.

"Greetings," I said, holding my arms out.

Turned out, these fellas were more the *whack you with giant gooey tentacle blob arms, ask questions later* types, rather than the *take me to your leader* variety.

With the wind knocked out of me thoroughly, they unceremoniously threw me into the portal, which was now a slightly different color than it had been a second ago, and hopped in after me.

Chapter 18

When I landed, it was blessedly not as hard as the last time I dove feet first off a cliff into an alien portal.

Though it was definitely not pleasant. I landed face first, belly-flop style, onto one of the giant, bean-bag alien blobs, and it let out what I can only describe as a wailing fart and rolled me off of itself.

"Look dude, I didn't want to land on you either," I said, retching and scrambling to get away, but there was practically nowhere to go.

We were in what looked like an airlock, based on my super scientific rocket travel background, which relied heavily on how many times I'd binged BSG. The blob things, which I really hoped I wouldn't have to spend so much time with I'd need to I learn their names, filled up most of the space and were clearly having some sort of heated discussion with one another. Their voices were garbled and angry, and they seemed to grow different appendages when the feeling struck, so I really couldn't tell how many limbs they had.

Eventually they came to some consensus, though, because they all three turned toward me.

I was trying to decide if I should cower or make myself big like when you get attacked by a bear. Splitting the difference, I cowered and also shook my cane at the nearest alien. "Stay back! I come in peace!"

One of them pushed a button on the wall near what I hoped was a doorway into some place with oxygen and not space vacuum, and over an intercom, I heard it say, "Come with us, human youth."

"You speak English?" I asked, eyes wide.

And the thing, which didn't even have visible eyes, somehow managed to roll them at me. Cool. I was hoping creatures would find me as insufferable up here as they did on Earth.

It pressed the button again, and the voice said, "Cause. No issues."

"Roger that," I said and gave a salute. "But can you tell me what's going on? Where are we going?"

I'm pretty sure it sighed and then added simply, "Negative."

"Fine, I get the picture. Don't have to tell me twice." I stood, wiping some of the excess blob goop off my trousers. At least I was dressed like a suave badass, so when my spaced corpse was found a billion light years from now, I'd look truly dapper.

To my surprise and delight, they didn't seem like they were going to kill me instantly, though, and after walking through a short, narrow hallway, they opened another door and pushed me through.

Yeah, it was definitely a jail.

I'd been in space for a whole four minutes and was already in trouble. Seemed about right.

"I'm definitely going to die here." I moaned and knocked my head against the closest wall.

The ceiling and back wall looked like those huge, plaster tiles in old elementary schools, while the wall facing the center of the brig was clear plastic. Maybe I could push through the tiles and escape. Though the seams appeared to be thoroughly sealed and yet somehow drippy and not anything I'd be able to pry apart or smash to bits with my cane.

I was a few tiles into tapping my cane across the ceiling, brown drips and all, when a scoff came from behind me, and I whirled around.

"Whoa!" I said.

Whatever it was looked at me with wide eyes, and my first, misplaced thought was that it was unfair that something so obviously not human could have the same withering eye judgment as my eighth-grade algebra teacher.

"Get back!" I yelled, and I held my cane out as a weapon, twirling it around and yet again wishing I'd gone for one like my grandma has, with a jabby spike at the bottom.

Once I had gallantly climbed up onto the bench with the cane ready to strike, I squinted in the cool dim light at the other prisoner. "Who are you?"

"Who are *you*?" they shot back. Fair enough.

"My name is Chuck," I said warily, looking across the room at the... "Alien," I blurted.

"Your name is Chuck Alien?" They looked at me with that same begrudging patience.

"What? No, I'm Chuck," I said, flustered. "You alien."

I was really grateful I'd met all of my best friends before anyone knew what it meant to be odd. Otherwise, I might never get anyone to talk to me more than once.

"Yes, me alien. You Chuck. Me good," they said with an uncanny Flintstones impression. This was getting stranger by the minute.

"Are you mocking me?"

"Yes." They looked me dead in the eye.

I let my guard down a bit at that and lowered myself back onto the bench. I decided it was safe enough, given that we had two pretty solid barriers between one another, to sit for a second and take in the alien.

"Are you a prisoner too?" I asked.

They gestured around their cell. It was across the small room from me and we could see each other through the clear door facing the opening where the guards had brought me.

"Why are you in here?" I asked before realizing that might be horribly rude. "Sorry, I haven't met many aliens. Or prisoners. I hope that wasn't rude?"

"Don't worry. I've seen every episode of *Friends*. Nothing you say will shock me."

"*Friends*? Really?"

"You're not a fan?"

"I mean, it got outdated pretty dang fast. And it's super white. And transphobic, at times. Not to mention Jennifer Aniston is kinda the most blah human to ever make everyone think she's amazing. Though Paul Rudd was a fantastic addition toward the end."

"My name is Axa, by the way." They laughed. "And I haven't actually seen every episode of *Friends*. I just know that almost all humans have an opinion about it."

I laughed. "I guess that's true. I really am Chuck, by the way. Human. Of planet Earth. She/her pronouns."

"Axa. Taurine. She/her pronouns work best for me in human speech patterns. Though I'm what you might refer to as gender fluid." She held her hand up like she was going to give a wave or a high five.

I mimicked the gesture, and it seemed to please her.

We both sat quietly for a few moments. And I took a few breaths. I was beginning to wonder just how long I'd been stuck in here because my meds were definitely wearing off.

"So, do you mind if I ask what you're in here for?" I was hopeful it was okay and also hella curious.

"Oh, you know, the usual saving-the-galaxy shit," she said with a flip of her wrist.

I couldn't help but laugh. But the look on her face, which I was just now really looking at, made it seem like she was being serious.

"Wait, what? Really?" I asked.

She smirked at me. Even while she was sitting down, I could tell Axa was tall and thin. Not creepy, Slenderman tall and thin but like a super lean, super tall basketball player. Her skin was smooth and had a bluish tint to it. There were enchanting freckles along the side of her face and down her arms.

She wore a skintight, white-and-green, short-sleeved jumpsuit that had straps like overalls. There was a reptilian look to her, and her eyes were almost completely black, from what I could tell. Her hair was bright, neon blues and greens, and it was in a huge, full braid down the middle and shaved on the sides. The undercut of punk rock dreams.

"Well, of course I was saving the galaxy. Isn't that why you're in here?" Axa asked back at me.

"I mean, no. No, I'm just trying to save my friends," I said, feeling deep in my gut that I had definitively bitten off more than I could chew. Which was honestly something I probably should have concluded before being captured by aliens, but hindsight was twenty-twenty. *So lay off, brain.*

Also, I decided I probably shouldn't think about it too much since my brain had the tendency to get in really doom-focused loops, especially when I didn't have my meds.

"Sometimes saving our friends and saving the galaxy looks like the same thing," Axa said with a small smile.

"You haven't seen a medium-sized brown human boy around, have you? Short black hair? Puerto Rican?" I asked, suddenly hopeful I might just luck out. I mean, how many galaxy saving aliens were around anyway?

"Not that I can say," she said. And my face must have fallen because she looked away as though embarrassed for me.

"Oh," I said, suddenly feeling very lost and very tired. "I'll have to just keep looking then. I technically only just recently got started. May as well keep going. Also, I might be in trouble with those big ugly blobs too."

"Yeah, that's what usually gets you thrown into a Phuphrath prison cell. What did you do to piss them off?"

"It was more of a wrong place, wrong type sort of thing?"

"Odd." Axa went silent and still for a few minutes. I thought maybe she had fallen asleep, but then she spoke. "What is your friend's name?"

"Samuel," I said. "But we all call him Ghost."

At that, she sat up straighter. "Ghost?"

"Yeah, have you heard of him?"

"We have many agents throughout the galaxy," she said cryptically. But we'd just met, and I didn't want to press her for more information. I was guessing aliens who ran around saving the galaxy couldn't just blab about whatever whenever.

"I might be able to help you reunite with your friends." She slid forward a bit. "But not while we're in here."

"Not being in here anymore works for me. What do you have in mind?"

Chapter 19

Turned out, hatching an escape plan with an alien on a spacecraft was not in my present skill set, but we were getting to know each other, so there was that. Axa was way more experienced at such interplanetary craft issues than me, and so I took her *wait and see what we can learn* lead.

"Really, though, how are you speaking English?" I asked.

The aliens who had taken me captive seemed to only make hiss, blub, and sputter sounds unless they were using the ship's translator, but Axa could have gotten a job as a news anchor. Her speech was so precise. She had a vibrating underlying tenor to her voice that made it seem slightly inhuman, but I did not understand how she could communicate with me so easily.

"I studied?" she said, like it was the most obvious thing in the world.

"Wait, you took English classes?"

"Yes. It took me a long time to get to this part of the galaxy, you know. Had to find ways to pass the time."

"How did you learn it? Is it hard? Is it way different from your own language?"

"Not any harder than a lot of languages. At least our vocal cords function in pretty much the same way. It's not much different from some other human dialects though."

"Wait, human dialects? So, you speak, human, not English."

"Well, yes, of course, that's kind of egocentric of you to assume I'd only learn how to communicate with American humans."

"If that's the most America-centric thing you encounter, I'll feel like I'm a pretty good Earth ambassador. Though it pains me that you really have seen so many episodes of *Friends.*"

"Not just *Friends.*" Then she rattled off essentially all of TBS and Nick at Night programming for the past forty years.

"Wow, so you're telling me that you are totally addicted to television," I said. "I'd kill for some TV right about now."

Just then, the lights dimmed about twenty percent. Our cells were relatively bare, and the lighting was embedded in the walls and ceiling. Several times a day, the lights would change color to simulate the time of day.

"On interstellar ships, it's important to keep sleep cycles regular, no matter how long you've been in space," Axa had explained. Unfortunately, the Phuphrath kept significantly shorter days than we did, based on how quickly the lights switched from day to night and back.

It was fine with me because I prefer napping anyway, which drove my parents up the wall, but it was straining on Axa and she got sort of grouchy when the lights rose and interrupted her sleep. "On my home planet, we have nights that last similar lengths to those on Earth. This eight-hour rotation is making me sick."

I tried not to think too hard about a planet spinning around that rapidly and shoveled some of the nutrient bar that came through a sliding metal door in the wall. Each time it opened, I tried to get a look inside, but it just looked like a blank box.

"I guess we should feel lucky it doesn't taste bad?" I replied, munching on it. Water was dispensed in bags attached to the wall. It was like drinking out of one of those travel pouches but guinea pig style.

I was also grateful that there was a place to go to the bathroom that resembled a human toilet close enough that I wasn't too confused and didn't need to ask for help.

I was even more grateful that privacy was a more universal norm than I would have thought, so every time you activated the toilet, the windows fogged. You couldn't take too long though, or the windows would clear up. Let's just say Axa and I were getting to know each other. Very well.

"Yes, luckily it does not taste bad." She finished her own portion.

"And they must not want us dead because we would already be, right?"

"Yes, that is my assessment as well. But how long we've been moving makes me think we're being transported, and I'd much rather stay in the same solar system as my ship." Axa sighed and looked at her wrist for the thousandth time.

"This is such a rip-off." I threw the remnants of my nutrient bar back into the hatch and took a drink from the water pouch.

"What is?"

"I'm literally in space. In a spaceship. And I don't get to see outside, like at all. Not even for a second. This is totally not fair. How am I supposed to take in the wonders of the galaxy from here?"

"Prisoner holding cells on ships have universally unpleasant views." Axa closed her eyes and leaned her head back.

"Been in a lot of cells?"

She opened one eye a crack then closed it again. "Let's just say more than one."

"Ooo. A lady with a past," I said, waggling my eyebrows at her.

She snorted and said, "Not exactly a lady, but sure, that sounds like me."

"Seriously though, tell me what I'm missing." I laid down on the bench cot.

"It depends on the sector. But lots."

"Can you tell me about where you're from?"

"I could. But it's been a long time since I was there, and I'd rather not dwell on it right now."

"I can respect that."

She nodded in acknowledgment.

"Would you like to tell me a story from Earth?" she asked.

"One time, Corrin really needed to finish a book series, and because it was a snow day, we weren't in school. It was the only time she basically threatened us with dissolving our friendships if we didn't go with her to get the next one."

"She sounds like an avid reader," Axa said.

"Sometimes you use words that make you seem British," I commented, completely losing my train of thought for a few moments. "*Anyway*, we wound up reading for most of the morning, and when we left, Corrin actually logged into the library computer and checked out the book she was taking."

My face warmed at the memory. Corrin was basically the human embodiment of the precious eyes emoji.

"That is a cute story," Axa said. "Also, I really wish they'd give *us* something to read."

"I'd even take *The Great Gatsby* at this point," I agreed.

"I may not want to describe where I am from, but if you'd like, I can describe where I'm assuming we are being taken and the most probable views outside of the hull right now."

"That would be great!" I leaned forward, and Axa described the stars flashing past us and planets coming into and out of view. Vast expanses of nebula and slight course changes to avoid asteroid belts.

"We would have left Earth's solar system within the first few minutes of being on board," she said. "It would have been a pinprick quickly, though you would still get to see it because spaceships have to limit the fuel burn so close to a planet. Humans may not give a shit about their planet's atmosphere, but even the worst of us out here at least know we need habitable planets in general."

"Makes sense." I wished more than anything I could look outside. "I really hope I get to see space before I get thrown into an alien world prison forever."

"Me too."

"Zero gravity would be fun too."

"Sure, until you have to poop."

"Did you just make a potty joke? Axa! I'm aghast."

She smiled, pleased with herself. "I debase myself to keep your spirits up, my friend."

If I had to be stuck in a Phuphrath prison, at least I'd made a hot alien friend willing to make poop jokes. Things could definitely be worse.

Over the next few days, we tried to get any information from the Phuphrath, but they were silent for the most part and just checked on us every couple of hours with grunts. I thought I was learning to tell them apart from one another though, and I was fairly certain I would be able to point out their eyes if I needed to. I figured that knowledge could come in handy if I needed to jab at one of them.

They left us alone otherwise, which was probably good, but also meant they weren't telling us anything about our destination or why they had captured us to begin with.

Axa and I had been trying to figure out what sort of escape we could attempt, but everything involved stealing a ship of some sort, which was obviously making things more difficult since I had less than zero experience with ships, let alone stealing and/or flying one.

"That is a terrible plan." Axa shook her head.

I was standing in my cell doing stretches, while we brainstormed escape plans. Axa and I were taking turns mirroring each other's movements to try to stave off boredom and keep our muscles from getting too tight from sitting still all day. The moves relied heavily on *Avatar: The Last Airbender*. I was actually being more consistent exercise-wise than I had been all semester. A positive side effect to being stuck in an eight-by-ten-foot cell all day with zero access to streaming services. "Isn't there a basement we could use?"

"What's a basement? " Axa crossed her arms and scowled. Her eyes narrowed into slits. She was not used to human words she didn't know the meaning of.

"A basement is like a level underground," I said.

"You do remember we're in space, right?" she asked.

"Well obviously." Though I still had trouble wrapping my head around the fact that up and down were totally relative. "My friends and I used to sneak out of and into school through the basement."

"Well, there are no basements in space," Axa said.

"Well there are lower levels, so why don't you think it will work?" I asked.

"For starters, our captors are really stupid. But not that stupid."

"Well, that's one thing." I slumped back. "Why not use one of the portals like before?"

I knew the basics of using those at least.

Step one: jump, fall, or be tackled into it.

Step two: be at a new place.

"I doubt the one the Phuphrath have would take us anywhere we'd want to go. We'd most likely just end up on another one of their ships, now that we're so far from Earth." She'd been patiently explaining things to me for the last couple of days. I didn't think I was her first baby alien to encounter, so she was being very nice.

Plus, there was a *lot* of new information to process. I was trying to focus on the parts that made an impact on our current situation, but sometimes I just begged Axa to go on and on about the different types of little alien critters that existed.

Imagine red pandas but with antennae. I mean, it couldn't get much cuter than that. I wanted one. She told me they were super deadly, but I would still make one my pet. I would. I'd buy it tiny sweaters, and it would love me.

"It wouldn't love you," she had said.

"It will," I had insisted.

Axa brought me back to the present. "There are several types of portals and aliens like the Phuphrath use them to make short jumps, usually just from planet to ship. They're kind of like escape hatches."

"So then, where did Pacey and Corrin end up?" I asked. "And I guess that's what happened to Ghost too."

"Hopefully, your Pacey knew where they were headed and what ship they would end up on or at which base."

"They definitely believed they knew where they were going. They said it was the same place Ghost had been and that they had a contact there."

"That's hopefully what happened. Not too many species use the portals, and they wouldn't want to wind up on the wrong ship or in the wrong place."

"Can't be worse than this one." I rolled my eyes up at the bare ceiling.

Axa snorted. "I mean, it could have just led to open space."

"What!" I yelled and almost fell over from my really authentic water bending pose.

"But they're probably completely fine," Axa said quickly and put her hand up against the glass window. She told me that her people would hold their palms together when they wanted to comfort or calm one another. Sort of the equivalent of a side hug or a pat on the shoulder but in the shape of a slow-motion high five.

I put my hand up to the glass from across the holding cells.

For whatever reason, these aliens were not into refilling my generic Zoloft prescription, so I was a few days deep into some less manageable than usual anxiety. I mean, on top of all the situational anxiety, I would be slowly becoming a mess, even if I was just in my own neighborhood. Thanks, generalized anxiety disorder.

Axa was already learning how to help me manage things though. The regular exercise and lack of junk food and caffeine was helping too, but I hoped we'd be back by a pharmacy soon.

"They could be in big trouble though." I took a breath then returned to the stretches.

"Yes, they could be in big trouble," she agreed, resuming the exercises with me. "Even if they tracked down Ghost's contacts, they are not always welcoming to random drop-ins from strangers, so I hope your Pacey knew who they were reaching out to."

"You know a lot about these contacts of Ghost's." I crossed my arms, studying her.

"Saving galaxies. You meet people." She brushed it off.

"I'm pretty sure you're here on purpose to rescue me," I said. "Yeah, that would make sense."

"That does not make sense."

"All the more reason to bust outta this joint then. I'm not making any sense."

Then there was a loud hissing noise, like the air getting purged on a plane. And several clanks rattled the sides of the ship, which bumped up and down a few times before feeling solid again. I grabbed the side of the wall to keep from losing my balance.

"What was that?" My voice shook.

We'd been in deep space for so long it was incredibly jarring to be jostled around at all. I didn't realize how quiet the ship had been until now and how little it felt like we were moving. I'd gotten used to the steady, quiet hum and almost no other noises. Now everything felt foreign again, and I re-

remembered I was on an actual spaceship in actual outer space and had almost no idea what was going on.

Axa listened carefully to the noises. "We may not need that escape plan after all."

"What's going on?" I asked, trying to keep my voice from shaking.

She looked at me from across our cells. "Either we just docked somewhere, or someone is boarding this ship."

And at that, all the lights in our cells went out.

Chapter 20

"You freaking glow in the dark," I practically shrieked. The trails of dots and lines that ran from her forehead down her neck and arms were softly glowing a sea green, the colors moving around subtly, making it impossible to look anywhere else.

In the sudden darkness, Axa was all I could see for a few seconds, and then some dark red lighting turned on along the ceiling, flashing a slow, pulsing pattern.

"How did I not know you glowed in the dark?" I wished I had tried to be subtle and not stare, but I was straight up ogling her. She was interesting to look at *before* I knew she glowed in the dark. Now Axa was downright mesmerizing.

"I don't always." She looked down at her arms sounding somewhat embarrassed.

"What do you mean?"

"It's like a built-in rescue beacon. So you can be found in the dark if you're in danger. Doesn't exactly work for defenses, but where I came from, getting lost was the bigger threat."

I knew I should be focusing, but all I could think of was, "Oh my god your skin is Sting."

"What? No, what's a sting?"

"Not 'a,'" I said. "*The* most iconic weapon in all of fantasy."

"I don't technically know what that is." Axa stood and moved to the door of her cell, trying to see toward the doorway. "But based on your tone, I'm going with—that's not what this is."

"Hold on. So, you weren't totally feeling the instinct to be rescued until now?"

"Of course not, the Phuphrath are pretty useless."

"Well, that would have been nice to know since I've been freaking out this whole time." I mean, I was still going to be afraid of them, but I might have slept a little easier if I'd known that.

"It's probably better if you are not too relaxed."

There was more banging from somewhere in the ship, and we quieted down, listening to the sound of metal on metal.

"What do you think is going on?" I whispered.

"Put on your shoes," Axa whispered back, and we both bent to do that.

I sat on the bench and quickly laced them up then grabbed my cane and buttoned my vest and tuxedo suit coat. I ran my fingers through my hair and realized I probably should have been doing that for the last couple of days because they basically got stuck. I wasn't sure how much good I'd be for whatever was about to happen but putting on my shoes did make me feel less vulnerable. Thank goodness I'd gone with Converse and not heels.

The banging stopped, but the red lights kept pulsing bright and then dim. It reminded me of the tiny lights on the floors at movie theaters that are there to keep you from tripping when you hopped up during the film to grab a refill of popcorn. Or emergency exit lighting they always told you would show up on airplanes in case of evacuation.

"Should we be evacuating?" I asked.

"Be my guest." Axa shook her head at me, gesturing to our still very locked cell doors.

Hades, I hoped my charm was enough to convince her to let me tag along if she got out of here.

"Chuck, whatever happens next," Axa said, looking away from the doors to me, "Let me do the talking."

There was a hiss, and the doors slid open. Three humanoids walked in, decked head to toe in what I would guess was motorcycle gear. Okay, probably it was spacesuits, but they looked like a hard-core biker gang. Shiny, skintight black leather material, but in a steampunk fantasy sort of way. Lots of tubes and utility belts and what were definitely large space guns. They wore solid black helmets. The surface of the glass across the front was perfectly polished and smooth, reflecting the red lights, and making the reflections look like rows of glowing eyes.

I made a mental note to ask Axa if space motorcycles were a thing the next time we had a free moment. Then I hoped I wasn't about to die with my last thoughts being about whether space motorcycles were a thing.

One of them stepped over to a panel in the wall and waved a communication device of some sort over it, and a panel opened up. They hit a couple of buttons, and the lights came back on. To my astonishment, the doors to my cell slid open, and one of the space bikers beckoned me forward, arm outstretched.

"Um, I think I'm good right here," I said and backed up a step. Yep, I was definitely choosing the blobby brown aliens I knew kept me fed with delicious—okay, tolerable—space granola bars than these obviously bounty hunter assassin aliens.

It took two steps closer and reached out its hand again then spoke in a synthetic robot voice through a speaker in its helmet. "I'm Luke Skywalker. I'm here to rescue you."

"What the hell?" I said.

Still in the same, *passed through a radio speaker twice* voice, it said, "No, silly, your line is: 'Aren't you a little short for a Stormtrooper?'"

And it gestured toward me in a *come on, you can do it* sort of way.

"Aren't you a little short for a Stormtrooper?" I asked. Because things couldn't get weirder.

"Close enough, though I had hoped you would have gotten a little more into it," it said. Then it reached up and took off its helmet.

The Dora shook its long blonde hair out from the helmet in a way that was straight out of an episode of *Baywatch*.

"I fucking *knew* it," I said.

"You were right," the Dora said and reached out to pat my cheek. "I'm an alien, and I'm here to rescue you so you can be my bait."

"Wait, what?"

"Come with me. I'll explain," said the Dora.

But I didn't move. I trusted it even less now, though if you'd asked me the week before, I never would have thought that was possible. None of this was even in the realm of giving off positive vibes.

"Can Axa come too?" I nodded toward where she stood, no longer glowing, but looking intently back and forth between us.

The Dora looked her up and down then nodded and swiped its wristband over the controls, opening up Axa's cell as well.

"But we're going to need to take your communicator." The Dora cleared its throat and gestured to Axa's watch.

A brief scowl crossed over Axa's face, but she unclasped the band and handed it over.

"Thanks, doll." The Dora winked because of course.

We left the brig together and turned down the same passageway I'd come through when I first got onto the Phuphrath ship. How many days ago that was, I did not know, because my cell phone battery had died almost immediately since I never remembered to plug it in and hadn't anticipated needing my charger for a long space journey.

As we were leaving the cells, Axa took hold of my elbow gently and leaned in, bending down so she could whisper, "Do you know this alien?"

"I mean, sort of, but I don't like it."

"Don't trust it."

I whispered back, "No shit, Sherlock, it just said I was bait."

Seeming to consider me warned, Axa nodded and let go just as the Dora turned around.

"This way, you two," it said

And just like that, I got to see space. Like for real life, outer space. I had no idea where we were, which was pretty much my baseline for the duration of my time off planet, and much of my time on Earth, but it was breathtaking.

There were two planets, nearly side by side, looming in the view we had from a large window that ran along the wall. One looked a lot like Earth, browns and greens and blues. The other was mostly purples and reds. We were close enough to it to see giant crimson seas and rocky mountains that were black and shiny and speckled with long streaks of purple, mauve, and magenta. Each one had several moons as well, which hung like holiday lights around them.

There were ships in orbit around everything. Some were big and bulky, like the International Space Station. Others zipped around like tiny cars.

I looked for space motorcycles.

I did not see any.

Based on what I could see of our ship, we were somewhere in between, size-wise.

"Where are the big blobby guys?" I expected to see them around the ship. They were pretty difficult to miss after all.

"The Phuphrath have been dispatched," the Dora said matter-of-factly and gestured toward the nearest window.

Sure enough, there they were.

Frozen blob monsters drifted slowly away from the ship. Those things were so gross, and the vacuum of space did not improve their look. But I didn't think they planned on killing me. Regardless, I thought I might puke.

"Rather bold of you to 'dispatch' them so close to Planet Berth 60E6." Axa had taken on a posture even more upright than usual and was clasping her hands behind her back with an air of authority I couldn't muster even if Julie Andrews herself gave me lessons.

The Dora waved its hand dismissively.

"It was an unfortunate accident. General Nikaids gave the orders." And with that, its face shifted into that of a much older person with wrinkles and gray hairs then right back to its familiar teenage femme look.

"I *knew* it," I exclaimed. "I knew your skin was too clear to be true."

"Yes, obviously I wasn't going to give myself acne," said the Dora, clearly pleased with itself. I couldn't blame it. That was a solid *high school can always be worse so why make it harder for yourself* move.

"How long have you been embedded with the humans of Earth, impersonating one of them?" Axa asked.

I did not like the sound of the word "embedded," and while I was partly gloating to myself about how I knew the Dora was an alien before everyone else, I was also starting to feel more and more uneasy. The Dora had yet to extrapolate on exactly what it meant by "bait."

"Long enough to find out what we were looking for was already gone," the Dora said.

"So why bother with this human?" Axa gestured at me.

I was not liking the way these folks were talking around me, but also, I really wasn't quite sure how to join in on the chat. But I was getting the feeling that Axa at least had my back, so I was zero to one on alien allies.

Let's just say, if I had to choose, I'd go with glow-in-the-dark jail-pal alien over evil Kristen Bell one, whether I was friends with her or not.

"She is a person of interest," the Dora said, "and a viable way for me to gain access to an asset."

"You mean Ghost?" I blurted out, and Axa gave me a please-shut-up-Chuck glance. I would recognize that look a mile away.

"Yes, Chuck, I do mean 'Ghost.'" The Dora turned and looked at me, unblinking. "Though that is not the name my people refer to him by."

"And what name is that?" Axa asked.

The Dora snapped its head back her direction. "I'm beginning to wonder if your incessant questions are going to bother me enough to not bring you along."

Axa hunched over and mumbled an apology, almost instantly masking her confidence and authority with embarrassment.

The Dora ate that shit up. "We will be transferring you both off this vessel and taking you to one of our ships. Do you have any belongings to collect?"

"Nope," I said, patting myself down. "Think I've got it all here."

"Follow me," the Dora said then, looking at Axa, added, "you too."

"I'm fine with you just dropping me off at the nearest station," Axa said. "Really, no need to trouble yourself dragging me along."

"What the heck, Axa? Et tu, Brute?" I gasped and held my hand to my heart like it was breaking.

"I do not know what that means," Axa said.

"Oh, so Latin isn't on your Human language app?"

"Chuck, shush," said the Dora. Then it turned to Axa. "You'll come with us as well. We'll make a party out of it." Then it gave one of those lifeless, shit-eating grins. I physically shuddered, and it narrowed its eyes at me. "Come on, no need to dilly dally."

Chapter 21

B elieve it or not, ships across the galaxy were not made with universally matching hatches, so Axa and I were following behind the Dora through a clear tube that stretched from one spaceship to another. There was no gravity, so we were literally floating through space, and I could see in every direction, the view only broken up by a metal ring every couple of feet, each with a small handle we could pull ourselves along with.

"Okay," I said gaping. "Is this safe, though? Why do they have space suits and we don't? Are we going to be all right?"

I was trying to embrace the whole out-of-ship experience, but it was really not what I had envisioned.

In one direction there were the giant planets I'd seen from the other ship. In the other direction was just *space* space. Like actual, real space. Endless stars and blackness. With spaceship traffic zig zagging across our view.

We got to take a good look at the ship the Phuphrath had been holding us on. It was bulky and, to be frank, really ugly. A pieced-together blob of a ship to match the blobby blobness of our previous captors, and not in the endearing way rag-tag groups of space bandits always had on TV shows from the early 2000s.

Portions of it looked like they were specifically designed to be evil looking. Maybe that was the point, to look as menacing as you can? I tried to take it all in so I could ask Axa about the different sections later. It felt both bigger and smaller than I had expected it to be. I reminded myself that it was my first spaceship ride, so it was okay if I didn't have a total grasp of the situation.

We'd spent so much time in our cells, I didn't quite know how to process the size of it. Space was so trippy.

This was something completely different. Tiny ships zoomed around, and twice, enormous ships passed by, big enough to block out the light from the sun in this system. A ship would look really tiny, then it moved closer and was actually like Enterprise-D size.

I pictured a ship slamming into one of the ships we were floating between. I really didn't want to die in a space tube. "Do we have to worry any of those will hit us?"

"This area of space is regulated enough that we shouldn't have to worry about that too much," Axa said in a way she clearly believed was reassuring.

I did not feel reassured.

She seemed at home and kept gently nudging me back the right direction when I'd get distracted and let go of the handholds. We were moving slowly enough that even when I did bounce off one side of the tube, I didn't pick up enough momentum to really slam into the other. The problem was that I wanted to look in every direction simultaneously.

But then I started thinking about how far I would go before stopping if that wall wasn't there. But also, that wouldn't really matter because I'd be dead long before I could even appreciate that I had been worrying with good cause.

I read an article once about how, in astronaut training, they got locked in a completely empty room and had to fold one thousand origami cranes before they're allowed to get out. It was probably to make sure they wouldn't get into ADHD brain loops that were catastrophic and totally unproductive, and the more I kept thinking and looking, the more I was beginning to realize I might not actually be made for space travel.

"Hey, you look a little green." Axa grabbed my arm gently and pulled me beside her. "Close your eyes, and I can help you the rest of the way if you need."

"No," I said, taking a deep breath. "I can do it."

"Okay," Axa said, "We're almost there." The entire passage was probably only three hundred feet long. "Just follow me, and we'll be through it before you know it."

I wasn't sure why, but she moved in front of me.

But then I puked, and so I was thinking she actually saw that coming and wanted some distance between us before I vomited.

Nothing but nutrient bars all up in that space tube.

I noticed she didn't warn the members of the Dora's crew who were bringing up the rear.

Thankfully, we were indeed almost out of it, and because zero gravity was a sight to behold, I managed to keep away from most of the sick. We all reached the airlock on the opposite end a few moments later, me with my eyes closed the last few feet. I was assuming the two members of the Dora's team who were behind me weren't pleased, but their biker gang helmets were down so I couldn't see the glares they were certainly shooting my way.

The Dora's ship was about as different from the blob ship as it could get. Same spacey vibes straight out of a sci-fi movie. As in, tubes and stuff, but this one was way sleeker.

When we got inside, the Dora handed me a pouch with water, which I gladly took a sip of as I looked around.

"Of *course* you have the Apple Store version of a spaceship," I said, my lip curling at the Dora who was taking its helmet off and somehow had perfect hair even when it was floating everywhere.

"I don't know what that means." The Dora looked around as everyone oriented themselves to be standing on the same portion of the floor. There were small loops on the ground, and they gestured to me to put my feet into the holes.

"Neither do I," Axa said, taking a position next to me and putting out her elbow for me. I wasn't totally sure what was about to happen, but I assumed it was going to be gravity related.

"Just, you know, pearly white." I paused. "And shiny? Lots of graphics. Like thirty percent more graphics than that last ship. At least." Clearly no one understood, and why they would get every *Friends* reference but not know what an Apple Store aesthetic was did not make sense.

But the point was, this ship was sleek. Smooth, clean interior, and all the panels were touch screens.

I didn't even want to breathe too hard on any of the clean surfaces. I was really glad I did all the throwing up before we got inside the ship. I needed to find out if there was such a thing as a space Roomba or Merry Maids. That would explain why things were so devoid of smudges.

There was a low hum. Slowly, artificial gravity engaged, and we lowered to the floor. I was glad for the toe loops and for Axa's arm steadying me as we settled in and got oriented within the ship.

"Anyway," the Dora said. "Follow me and don't touch anything."

"I wouldn't dare," I said, meaning it.

We walked along a pristine hallway and into an area of the ship that looked like a large conference room.

"Sit." The Dora gestured to two chairs.

There was a shiny white—of course—table that I could see my reflection in. I quickly tried to sort my hair out of habit, when the Dora cleared its throat. It was standing with its arms crossed, looking very cross itself and eyeing me closely.

"Well, Chuck," it said, "it seems we have some things to discuss."

"Yes," I nodded, sagely.

"Feel free to begin talking any time."

"Um, I wouldn't just ask her to do that," Axa interjected.

"Hey! I have plenty of clever things to say," I said. "But honestly I'm pretty lost right now, so feel free to just chime in with anything you want to tell me about what you want me to tell you about."

"I actually followed that," Axa said. "We've been spending way too much time together."

"Let me put it to you this way," the Dora said. "Your friends are in trouble. I need to find Ghost. You'll tell me how to do that, or I'll come up with other ways to convince you."

"I really don't know what to tell you," I said, beginning to get really frustrated. I didn't even know what it was looking for other than Ghost, and if I could find him, I would do anything to make that happen.

"It will be much better for your friends if we find them, rather than if they find us. Ghost is the one we want," it said, cracking its knuckles.

"Are you going for gangster, right now?" I asked. "Because I really do not know what to tell you, and I don't know how many times you need to hear me say that."

"I do not like waiting."

"Yeah, me neither. This frankly sucks, and if I could, I'd figure a way out."

"I will hurt your friends, Chuck. I promise you that."

This interaction was getting us nowhere, and I could tell it was getting frustrated too. Welcome to the club, chum.

"Fine, if you won't cooperate, we'll find more persuasive ways to handle this," the Dora said, standing. It pressed some buttons on the table ,and one of the panels on the wall slid open. Two of its goons came in, and it was clear we were being dismissed.

I really hoped it was to eat dinner or to a bed for a nap. And not to an open airlock.

Chapter 22

"So, I gather you know this Dora?" Axa asked.

They'd given us some sandwiches and somehow—trying to be grateful and not totally creeped out—the Dora knew what my meds were and had provided them. Was this the start of Stockholm Syndrome?

Axa was wandering around the edges of our bunk room, looking around for I wasn't sure what but probably an escape hatch of some sort.

"Um, yeah, kinda," I said, sitting down on the nearest bed. These bunks were clearly not made for humans, and I sank into it like a half empty waterbed. It wasn't unpleasant but also wasn't great.

"Do you mind elaborating?" she asked, and I caught a whiff of exasperation in her tone. She knew me well enough to know I maybe didn't really want to get into it.

"Do I have to?" I asked, cringing.

"You have knowledge of the being that is literally holding us captive. It would definitely be for the best if you told me what you knew about her."

"Well, we go to the same high school?" I realized how ridiculous that sounded at the same time I realized Axa may not know what a high school is. "A high school is..."

She held up her hand and cut me off. "I don't need to know the details of Earth's education system."

"Well, that's good because frankly it's a hot ass mess," I said, "At least in the US. It's a total train wreck."

"Anything else, Chuck?" she pressed. "About the one you call the Dora?"

"Also, it kinda asked me out on a date, and I sort of turned it down."

"Great." Axa ran her hands through her hair then across her face. "No wonder she made a comment about us sharing a bunk."

"We also never technically learned its pronouns," I said.

"Have you been referring to her as 'it' this whole time?" Axa laughed. "The Dora uses she/her pronouns, it's indicated on her identification badge."

"Well, how does anyone expect me to be able to read one of those? And it's not like she was wearing it around school. And what was I supposed to do, talk to her?" I asked, throwing my arms into the air. "She is *clearly* evil."

"That's definitely true." Axa finally stopped her pacing and took a seat on a bench opposite me.

I thought about everything the Dora had said before. "She might be one of the aliens Pacey said wanted to destroy the Earth? The ones Ghost is trying to stop?"

"Did the Dora arrive before or after Ghost went missing?"

"After, as far as I know, she showed up after he disappeared," I said, thinking back to the first time I'd seen the Dora. "Corrin would know for sure though. She knew her before I did because of all the artsy stuff."

"It's possible she used tech to make it seem like she'd been on Earth much longer than she had. She's obviously trying to draw Ghost out."

I rubbed my eyes and wanted more than anything to just curl up in a ball and hide or wake up in my own bed or, better yet, Corrin's warm reading nook. Yeah, that sounded perfect. She could read some old dead white guy class reading assignment to me, and I could doze off because they were kind of all the same and she'd give me a summary of the plot later anyway.

Maybe she'd cover me up with one of her quilts that she always found at estate sales and collected because she liked to imagine the thoughts of the people who were sewing them.

"*Dude*, you have *got* to focus, like just a little bit, please." Axa came over and snapped—yes, snapped—her fingers at me. "Where did you just go?"

"Some place way cozier than this one." I groaned, flinging my arm across my eyes.

"Your friends are in danger," she said, looking at me with a serious face.

"I know. Ghost is some sort of intergalactic fugitive," I started.

But Axa shook her head. "No, your other friends. The ones who were still at school with you."

"Corrin and Bailey?" I asked, sitting up. "Why?"

"Because if it's been the Dora's plan to use you as bait all along, you could all be implanted with a"—she paused as if trying to find the right translation for something—"Cralzod death timer."

"Excuse me, what?" I shrieked. "That does not sound good."

"It's not."

That got my attention, and Axa explained to me it was a countdown type of robot death machine that would go off if the Dora decided Ghost needed more motivation. It got implanted in the bait and would ka-pow if the target didn't get in line. It sounded like an episode of *24*, and I hated it.

"How do we know if they're infected with the death thingy?" I asked.

"They would need to have been in close enough proximity to one of the Cralzod for it to implant the device. But it would have been as easy as slipping it into a drink."

"Oh my gosh like an evil alien roofie?"

"Yes, but there are no immediate effects, only certain death at the press of a button."

"This is seriously fucked." Tears were actually close to coming, even after all I'd been through. Worrying about Corrin and Bailey hadn't been my biggest concern until now.

"You might have one implanted too," Axa said.

But I waved her off. "I didn't let the Dora get close to me for even a second if I could help it. She gave me the heebie-jeebies from the start."

"But your other friends?"

I shook my head. "Pacey would be fine, but Bailey and Corrin could have been implanted. How close does she have to get to do it?"

"Close, but not for very long."

"Oh crap nuggets, Bailey was going to the dance with her. He could definitely be in trouble." I was suddenly more nervous than I'd felt in days. "I didn't remember because Corrin had just told me right before the blobs showed up, but the Dora and Bailey were going to the formal."

"That would definitely give the Dora enough time. What about your other friend? Did they spend much time in close proximity to one another?"

"Yes," I said, remembering the art opening. "I knew I should have stepped in. Ugh, the Dora is the worst."

Axa glanced at her wrist for like the hundredth time.

"Why do you keep doing that? Missing your Fitbit?"

"I am accustomed to being in constant contact with my ship, and having my communicator taken is really bothering me," she said, rubbing at the spot. The Phuphrath had been too dense to take it from her, but the Dora hadn't overlooked something so useful.

"Your friends are in real danger, Chuck. We have to find a way to contact them. Now that the Dora took my watch, that option is no longer there."

"Wait, you were able to use that communicator before?"

She looked at me, brows furrowed. "I haven't been completely honest with you, Chuck."

"In a good way or a bad way?"

"Um, good?"

"What have you been keeping from me?" I asked, frustrated.

"I cannot tell you everything," she said, looking genuinely regretful.

"Why not?"

"Frankly, you tend to ramble. Often."

"Okay, well that's not untrue."

We sat there in silence for a minute. Then she held up her long hand, so I could press mine to hers. It was the first time we'd gotten to actually touch palms, and there was something really comforting about her cool skin.

"Can I trust you?" I wanted to ask a trillion questions, but I didn't know where to start except for there.

"Yes, Chuck," she said. "You can trust me."

"Okay."

"We need to find a way to get in touch with your friends before the Dora enacts whatever plan she has going."

"If Pacey and Corrin went through the same portal as Ghost, do you think they could be together?"

"Maybe, though it sounds like the Dora has Corrin and Pacey fairly well tracked, so that might not be such a good thing for Ghost. Hopefully, if your pal has contacts that overlap with Ghost like they led you to believe, they'll have been able to contact each other from there."

"Will Ghost know about the death timers?"

"It's hard to tell," Axa said. "We don't even know for sure they've been implanted. But I've had run-ins with the Cralzod before, and it is a common tactic of theirs in hostage situations."

"They have to be close to the Dora for it to work, right?"

Axa looked at me somberly. "Right. The Dora will need to be within proximity to set it off. Which is why using you as bait doubles her chances of getting Ghost to comply with her demands."

I got up and paced around the small room, nibbling on my sandwich. I hated the idea of any of them being dragged further into this nightmare. Then, I had an idea. "If I had a tracker on me, could you use it to track whoever was tracking me?"

"Well, Chuck," said Axa, and I knew she was about to explain something to me like I was four. "It would depend on the type of tracker. For starters, GPS only works on a planet, but there are other types too."

"How could you tell if it was working?"

"The same answer, Chuck. it depends. There is more than one type of…"

"Yes, trackers. I know things."

Pacey had said they'd put a tracker in Corrin's car and on me. It had only just now occurred to me that the one thing I take literally everywhere with me is my cane.

I sat down and grabbed it, looking it over. I popped the rubber slip guard off and examined the base. This one had a small metal panel across the bottom. I tried twisting it, but that didn't work. So, I pushed it in, and sure as shit, a small click sounded, and a cylinder popped out.

"May I see that?" Axa asked, and I handed over the tiny device.

She turned it over in her hands and looked at it closely. "Has this been on you the whole time?"

"Yeah, since we left Earth. Not totally sure when Pacey bugged me with it. I think it's just the GPS kind though."

"It actually looks very sophisticated." She held it to a light and ran her finger along the side.

"Do you think it can help them find us?" I asked, not sure if that was even what I wanted. Wouldn't it be safer for them to just leave me to my fate and stay as far away from the Cralzod as possible?

"Yes, and more importantly, I think it will help *us* find *them*. I can work with this."

"Right," I said, leaning into this *just gonna go ahead and trust her* mentality.

"Okay, I'm going to need some help with this." Axa sat down with me on the bed.

Then, I just watched in awe as she started pulling the tiniest bits of metal and wire and batteries from nowhere. Well, not nowhere. All over her tight overalls, there were small seams that looked sewn shut, but when she ran her fingers along them, they were open and had tiny tools she brought out one at a time.

"Can I use your jacket?" she asked. It would have been easier to work on the small table attached to the wall, but she needed to be ready to hide what she was working on when the Dora or one of her goons came in. So Axa used the jacket as a work area and lined up all her tools neatly.

It was like watching someone put together a Lego set. The way she pieced everything together was so swift and precise. She even pulled some pieces out of her giant braid, and the chain on her earring was a wire, and the back of the earring had a battery in it. Every once in a while, she would ask me to hold something still or hand her a tool. They reminded me of those lock picking kits magicians used. Or something a watchmaker would have. She used one of the tools to pick at part of the bottom of her boot and removed a long string of putty that, when water was added to it, sealed the various bits like a weld would.

At some point, the lights turned down, and she kept working in the near dark, her glowing skin lighting up the small device enough for her to keep going. "I won't be able to finish this tonight. But I'll work as fast as I can, Chuck. I thought we had more time before the Cralzod made this move."

"You want to tell me what you're working on?" I asked.

"A way to save your friends, Chuck. And, while we're at it, Earth."

Chapter 23

"Well, isn't this just adorable."
I cracked open an eye to see the Dora standing in the doorway to the small quarters Axa and I had apparently wound up cuddling in. If I wasn't super worried about dying at the hands of a maniacal Kristin Chenoweth doppelganger, I'd be a little more bashful about it.

Turned out Axa ran about ten degrees cooler than I did, and it was like sleeping on the cold side of the pillow all night. Plus, she glowed just a little bit, the same colors as the dimmed night lights in the cabin but in a moving, soothing way. Not to objectify her, but it was like snuggling with a soft, chilly lava lamp.

I wasn't sure where I stood on interspecies relationships, but I'd ten out of ten cuddle her again.

Wait, did I drool? Cool. I'm awesome. Anyway, I didn't want the Dora to think she had caught us off guard, so the two of us just sat up nonchalantly. Without looking, I felt my suit jacket still balled up against the wall of the bunk. It held the portal controller that Axa had worked on late into the night.

"Put on your shoes," the Dora said. "You're eating in the mess with the crew."

"I'm still confused. Are we prisoners?" I asked as Axa handed me my shoes and cane.

"Not so much prisoners but hostages," the Dora said. "I believe the Phuphrath were keeping you prisoner, but we're only needing you to get your friend to cooperate. If you make it out of this situation alive, you'll be free to have us drop you off at the nearest planet."

"Habitable planet?" Axa asked, a clarification I would not have even considered, and so I mentally added that to the growing list of why I needed to make sure Axa loved me.

The Dora turned unblinking and gave that devious cheerleader grin.

"Of course. If you play nice." Then she turned and walked away with a swish of her pony tail.

We followed, and as we got closer to the food, which I could smell, unlike the bland Phuphrath granola bars, I realized I hadn't eaten anything but that sandwich the night before since before I puked in the air tunnel. I wanted to get to planning some heroics, but we obviously couldn't do that while surrounded by the Dora and her crew, so might as well enjoy a meal.

Unfortunately, the food did not look nearly as good as it smelled. We were definitely eating some sort of cross between a jellyfish and space fungus, which my squeamish chicken nugget loving heart really wasn't into, especially for breakfast. It was pickled and then fried up in a microwave-looking oven situation. If they'd like chopped it up first, maybe I would have enjoyed it more, but this thing was whole and about the size of my forearm.

"Sit, get to know my crew," the Dora said. "I've been telling them *all* about you."

We sat where the Dora indicated, and no one said anything or moved as we did. They passed around the food, and everyone took portions of the Jell-O-fish thing and also what looked blessedly like rice and carrots on the side. I was given hearty scoops of everything and a strong glare when I tried to wave away the Jell-O-fish. So, like Riker on a Klingon field trip, I accepted a heaping spatula full.

All five of the crew sitting around the table looked human, but while three of them maintained the same appearance, two of them were constantly shifting faces every time I blinked or looked away.

"Pax-7, Brittina-0-9, cut it out, you're distracting our guest," the Dora said sharply, and they stopped shifting and settled on one appearance each.

"So, what's there to do for fun around here?" I moved the food around on my plate. I figured if I got myself distracted enough, I could get some of it down eventually.

"Allow me to lay out some ground rules," the one called Pax-7 said.

They had taken on the look of a middle-aged man with a beard and gray hair. Pax-7 didn't look like the grandfatherly type though. More like a pissed-off Billy Bob Thornton. I wondered what they looked like in their natural state.

"While you are on our ship, you will obey each of us. We will instruct you as we see fit. You will stay within your quarters or the designated eating area. The medical bay is off limits, the bridge is off limits, the cargo hold is off limits, the shuttle bay is off limits," he said, ticking the growing list of places off on his fingers.

"Okay, so, to clarify," I interrupted, "I can hang out on the bridge?"

They all looked at me with furrowed brows for a moment.

Then, the Dora leaned over. "It's called sarcasm. She isn't really that dense. Humans enjoy it as humor or entertainment."

This definition made the entire table look grumpier. And I really didn't like how much it felt like this was going to be a long-haul event. Did I really need to know the whole list of places I wasn't supposed to go? How long would we have to be here?

"Not fans of sarcasm, got it. From now on I'll use air quotes so you can tell when I'm being sarcastic. Would that be 'helpful'?" I put air quotes around the word helpful.

Silence. This was going to be a super fun imprisonment.

"Moving on," Pax-7 continued. "You will address us by rank—"

"I can already assure there is no way I'm going to be able to remember all of that." I said.

"Well, then, try," the Dora said, clearly exasperated.

"Wait, the Dora," I said, picking up a vibe. "Were you hoping this would go well? Are you introducing me to your *friends*?"

"Excuse me?" she asked, looking confused.

"Oh my god, you want your friends to like me," I said, jaw dropping. "The Dora, you liiiike me."

"I can assure you, that is not what is going on here." Brittina-0-9 scowled. The others just looked perplexed.

"Oh no, are you jealous?" I turned toward Brittina-0-9. "Sorry I always make things awkward."

"No, that is not what is happening," the Dora said.

"If you say so."

"I *do* say so."

"This is a waste of time," one of the others said, getting up and putting their plate into what looked like a dishwasher on the wall.

"No, don't get up, really," I said. "I want to get to know y'all. Let's play twenty questions. I can't pass up the chance to learn all about the Dora's pals. Does she have any special quirks I should know about? Guilty pleasures? Embarrassing elementary school stories?"

The Dora sighed and signaled to the others that they were free to get up and go about their spaceship duties. Axa was just sitting eating her alien lunch like we hung out on this ship every day.

I decided I should eat too and began to shovel the food in earnest, not thinking too hard about what it looked like.

Turned out it was *delicious*, especially after so many days of the bland nutrient bars.

The three of us sat and finished eating in relative silence. I'd either talked myself into exhaustion or my anxiety meds were starting to work again.

"As we were saying, just keep your hands off our ship, and we'll be fine," the Dora said. "I need you to help me draw out your friend. And when we do, which we will, I need it to go my way.

"He'll need to know you have me."

"Yes, we will send him a message, confirming your capture."

"Oh," I said, "like a proof of life selfie?"

"Yes, like a proof of life selfie. Ghost has stolen something from us, and we want it back. We are willing to exchange you and, of course, have other incentives in place."

I gulped down another bite. Those other incentives she was talking about were my best friends, and I was really getting tired of being part of some trading game. "What are you going to do when my friends come to get me?"

"We don't need them, just Ghost and what he stole." The Dora waved her hand dismissively. "Unless they become troublesome. Then I may be forced to dispatch them."

"And so, what makes you think I'll help you?"

The Dora sighed. "Obviously I'll kill you too if you don't comply." She gestured to Axa. "And your Taurine friend as well."

"Wow, you are really a mean alien. I do not like you." I mustered up as much stink eye as I could.

"Look, I tried to play nice. I tried to draw Ghost out through other methods, but he is playing hard to get and I am tired of not having what I need." She sat with her skinny, pale arms crossed and her perfect messy bun ponytail looking at me all smug.

"I thought we were friends," I said.

"No, you didn't."

"Okay, right, no I didn't. Nevertheless, this is next level bag of dicks."

Axa actually snorted at that, and we both turned to her.

"Sorry, please continue," Axa said.

"Ugh." The Dora stood up and grabbed both our plates.

"Hey," I protested. "I wasn't finished."

"Both of you back to your quarters. Brittina-0-9, escort them."

Apparently, Brittina-0-9 had been standing guard just outside because she came in with a sneer on her face and what looked like a Taser.

"I was actually wondering if I could do a spacewalk?" I said as Brittina-0-9 ushered us out.

Axa gave me a side-eyed look.

"What?" I shrugged. "I really want to do a spacewalk."

"If we make it out of this, I'll personally take you on a spacewalk." Axa patted my arm.

"Really?" I asked excitedly.

"Shh," Brittina-0-9 said. "No chit chat in the hallways."

I really was not a fan of this crew, I thought as we walked back to the quarters.

"If your idea was to chat them to death, I think it could work," Axa said when we were back in our room.

"I honestly haven't talked to anyone but you in so long, I was worried I had forgotten how to blab on and on. I just abhor a vacuum."

"We did actually get quite a bit of information about the size and layout of the ship, so that will be useful."

"I am really glad you're here with me, Axa." And I truly was. If she wasn't, I would've been so screwed.

"Well, don't be too glad yet. At least one of us has to get off this ship and warn your friends about the death bot trap." She took off her boots and started some of the same stretches we'd gotten into the habit of doing in the Phuphrath ship.

I joined in with the exercise, looking forward to nighttime when we could more safely make progress on the device. Mostly, though, I was feeling useless. I guessed that was to be expected of bait. But I was determined to do anything I could to get my friends safely on the other side of this shit-show.

The next few days and nights were pretty mundane, aside from the mortal peril and crash-course MacGyver training part. Axa and I settled into our exercise routines and upped our banter in the dining area because it so clearly bothered the rest of the crew. The Dora did her proof of life thing, which turned out to be a three-dimensional hologram that fit in the palm of her hand when she was finished scanning me.

She said I had to be talking for it to work authentically, and, of course, the only thing I could think to say was the Gettysburg Address for absolutely zero discernible reason. We'd had to memorize it for a history class in eighth grade, and it was literally the only words I could think of.

Other than what words were coming out of my mouth, it was actually really cool and reminded me of Princess Leia's hologram that came out of R2-D2.

Too late, I realized what would have been ten thousand times cooler than the freaking Gettysburg Address was— pretty much anything, but specifically—"Help me Obi-Wan Kenobi, you're my only hope." What was wrong with me?

I asked her if I could re-record it, and she just clicked her mouth at me. "No way. They will definitely know it's you when they watch this."

I really hoped the last words my friends heard me say wouldn't be "four-score and seven years ago."

We had to get from the Dora's ship to whatever vessel my friends had hopefully rustled up and intercept them before they walked into a trap and got close enough to hit the death bug button on Corrin or Bailey. We had no way of knowing whether my friends knew about the devices or that Corrin and Bailey needed to stay out of range.

It would be great to see my friends again, and we were hoping the circumstances wouldn't be so grim as the Dora had in mind.

But we had a plan too.

Chapter 24

One summer, we got really into blowing stuff up. Eventually it turned into a more productive, less destructive hobby via rocket making, but for a while, we took every opportunity we got to explode things. Axa's assessment that American teenagers are "the most reckless of all juvenile species" was solidified in her mind when I told her about it.

"I'm going to go ahead and stay back here" were the smartest words ever spoken in the Human language, and bless her, Corrin had probably said them about forty-three times that summer.

Based on this reckless teenager's expertise, I finally had a way I could help with the plan.

Blowing stuff up is dangerous. Blowing stuff up in a spaceship? *Really* dangerous.

So when, as part of the plan, I yelled, "Um, hello, I have a bomb," it got their attention. I just had to keep that attention long enough for Axa to power down the ship, power up the portal, and use the modified tracker and device to jump to where Pacey was based on my cane tracker, which was hopefully in range.

Easy peasy.

Everyone stood up quickly, and then the Dora said loudly, "Wait!" and held up her hand. The five or so members of the crew grew eerily still, and the Dora walked up to me slowly, hands raised, with what was probably supposed to be a reassuring, but came off as a totally condescending, grin all over her stupid pretty face.

"Don't come any closer." I held the plasma cutter we'd snatched up to the fuse.

It gave me a large amount of satisfaction to see them squirm a bit. Though the squirming was all metaphorical and in the vibes, not in actuality. Statuesque as ever. It bothered me to no end that I was the human embodiment of a fidget spinner and constantly surrounded by humanoid statues. It was unsettling, and I hated it.

"Chuck, sweetie, I don't know if you understand how this works," she said, looking around the cabin.

"Actually, I'm really super good at making bombs so..."

"I've never really gotten the bomb maker vibe off of you." The Dora stepped toward me.

"Take one more step, and I'll let 'er rip." I pointed to the pipe and fuse in my hand.

"Where did you even get that?" The Dora sounded genuinely curious.

"I made it. Didn't you know I'm super clever?" I actually had made it and can tell you how.

It was fake and therefore wouldn't get me on any watch lists. I was obviously not going to blow up a spaceship that I was currently inside of. We'd used some of the tools and metal that were left over after Axa finished the portal controller and rigged it with the tracker from my cane.

The Dora let out a snort.

And I added, "Hey, I resent the implication, you rat bastard."

"I just don't quite understand what you're trying to do right now," the Dora said. "Can you help me understand? You don't seem like someone who wants to die."

I realized I had lost track of timing this whole thing and had to start counting again in my head. I figured counting to one hundred twice would give Axa enough time, but who knew how long she'd had already. Better safe than sorry, so I kept going with the *look at me, I'm going to blow everyone up* charade.

Including "Chuck counts aloud in her head" as part of the plan was a pretty major oversight on our part.

"You don't know me," I said, shaking the pipe. "I want a lot of things."

"You're stalling, aren't you? That's not an actual bomb."

"You wouldn't want to test that though, would you?" I menacingly clicked on the handheld plasma cutter. But it didn't turn on. So, I tried it again and realized I probably should have asked Axa how it worked before we got things rolling. I hadn't planned on threatening to light it with the actual flame on.

The Dora rolled her eyes and crossed her tiny white arms at me.

"Okay, now I'm bored." She strode over to me, taking the pipe from my hand.

I supposed in hindsight, having a bomb that required you to light it wasn't the most dramatic thing, particularly if you couldn't get the lighter to work. But it still gave me a lot of satisfaction when she immediately took it to an airlock and spaced it. So, it was at least convincing enough for her to not just toss it down a garbage shoot.

"You two," the Dora barked at Brittina-0-9 and Pax-7, "go find Axa and see what the hell she is up to that made Chuck act so disruptively."

I made a move to go with them.

But the Dora held up a hand. "No, no, you can stay put."

It was definitely in one of the top twenty most tense four minutes of my life—look, I'd been having a really rough couple of days—but not too long after they left, Brittina-0-9 and Pax-7 returned and shrugged.

"She is in the bathroom." Pax-7 reported.

"Doing what, exactly?" the Dora asked.

"She is in the shower. Catag was guarding the chamber and has not left their post." Brittina elaborated. It would have seemed creepy, but they delivered the information so monotone that it just came across as mundane as if they'd just said, "doing her taxes."

"Phew," I said. Out loud. Because I am a horrible schemer.

"Expecting something else?" the Dora asked me sharply.

"What? No, that seems about right. She was getting rather stinky. So. As her bunk mate, I'm very glad she was showering. You know, during space travel, we really tend to neglect our own personal hygiene—"

The Dora held up her hand to cut me off. "Well then what, might I ask, were you doing with a fake bomb, Chuck?"

"First off, I resent the implication that I couldn't make an actual bomb. Because, for all you know, that one *was* real, and you just dodged a major bullet, missy."

"And second?" the Dora prompted.

"Oh, no, I was just wanting to get your attention."

Just then, the actual thing I'd been waiting for happened.

The ship lurched to a stop so quickly we all went tumbling forward, but right before we would have hit the ground, the artificial gravity turned off, so it was a bounce, not a splat.

Axa had essentially slammed on the brakes, giving Ghost time to catch up with us. Now she had to make it to the portal in the cargo bay and hope she was able to attune it to Pacey and therefore the portal on Ghost's ship.

On the bridge, everyone but me had their boot magnets turned on and found purchase on a surface. I, on the other hand, flew at the Dora, who caught me and stopped me from spinning into a wall.

The lights on the part of the ship we were in powered off and a warning blared.

"Hull Proximity Alert" repeated on all the speakers, and the entire crew jumped into action, moving to various wall panels and pulling on spacesuits. Axa warned me that would happen if she was able to power up the portal.

Then, as quickly as the alert began, it stopped.

There was a loud hum as the power to this part of the ship returned and both the lights and gravity came back online.

Carga came running down the hallway and burst onto the bridge. "The other prisoner is gone."

"What?" the Dora screeched.

Everyone was still frantically checking readings and tightening up their spacesuits. I noticed no one had bothered making sure I had one but whatever. I was going to assume it was a *put the mask on yourself before your aisle mate* type of moment.

"She wasn't in the bathroom. I don't know how she got past me," Catag said.

I knew how. It was an ole switcheroo.

Pax-7 looked up from one of the control panels. "A transport portal was operated out of the cargo bay. That must have caused the proximity alarm."

"Follow her!" the Dora screamed.

"We can't. It's been deactivated, and I'm locked out. It will be at least an hour before we can use it again."

The Dora yelled and punched a wall. I only thought people punched walls in movies. But sure enough.

Best-case scenario, Axa was able to portal hop onto my friends' ship and was currently filling them in on our situation and they'd be here to rescue me, keeping Corrin and Bailey as far away as possible in the meantime.

Worst-case scenario, the tracker didn't work, and Axa was who knows where.

Either way, the Dora was pissed.

Chapter 25

The Dora was angrier than I had ever seen her before, and she had Pax-7 take me to the actual brig, not the room Axa and I had shared. It felt a helluva lot lonelier without Axa and really hoped this plan worked. I laid down on the bench and tried to rest, daydreaming of not being alone on a hostile alien ship that had just become significantly more hostile.

So, I knew I just had to wait because, this time, I was the lobster Pacey made us all rescue from Red Lobster the summer they became vegan. And I didn't really know whether my friends would try to bust me out or go with the bribe-the-hostess method, but either way, I never doubted they were coming for me.

A million years later—I was not one for solitary confinement—one of the quieter of the Cralzod crew came in, grunted, and gestured toward the hall.

Thank goodness, because I was Chucking really hard. I was so glad for anything to start happening.

"Okay, so where are you taking me now?" I asked as they led me along the corridor back to another airlock where everyone else had gathered.

Like before, the crew was wearing their black spacesuits, but this time they'd given me one as well. I was still really hoping I'd get to do a spacewalk, and I figured if they were giving me a suit, I wasn't just getting pushed out an airlock. Axa had reassured me people rarely used that method as a punishment, but I wasn't going to let my guard down.

"Do I get to do a spacewalk?" and even through the shiny helmets, I could see they thought the question was ridiculous. Why was that like a universal response people had to my inquiries?

I swore every day of my life I was reminded that there were, in fact, bad questions. It was totally not my fault that there were a *lot* of questions to ask when you were in space, and now that my new best friend and ambassador to the cosmos, Axa, was gone, I had no one to ask.

I sighed and pulled on the black suit over nothing but my underwear because apparently this shit was skintight and made to order. It was lighter than I expected. You always see those videos of the first astronauts wearing suits that weigh like two hundred pounds, but it didn't matter because they were in zero gravity. Though I lamented leaving my tux behind, these suits were made to be both in space and in places with gravity and to transition between the two seamlessly. Also, I was certain I looked like a total badass. I wondered vaguely if they would let me keep it after whatever was about to happen.

After we were all suited up, they pushed me to the bridge, and we waited. Them shushing me as a group any time I started to speak.

Thankfully, I didn't have to wait too long to find out what was going on because the boring silence was broken up by the sound of another ship hailing us.

"Don't say a word," the Dora said.

She pushed the call button on the smooth communications control panel, and the screen came to life.

"My friends!" I squealed, when I saw who was on the screen, and the Dora shot a glare in my direction.

"She said to shush," Brittina snarled at me.

"Right, okay, sorry," I said and mimed locking my lips together.

Ghost was on the bridge of a ship, and Pacey was next to him, arms crossed, both looking very serious.

"General Dora, we finally speak face to face," Ghost said.

"Whoa, look at you with the high rank, the General," I said, giving the Dora a thumbs up. "I would have been able to remember that."

She ignored me. "Ghost of Earth, you have given us quite the hunt. I hope you have decided to give us what we're looking for."

"Right, so, that's a problem for several reasons. One, I don't like being threatened. And two, I definitely do not like when my friends are threatened."

"Ooo, y'all are in trouble," I said, smiling at Brittina. She was my least favorite, and I hoped Ghost had something special planned for her.

"We're happy to stop threatening them, if you just hand over the launch codes," the Dora said.

"Wait, launch codes?" I asked.

"Destroying Earth would be as easy as pushing a button. You humans have set yourselves up for this end," the Dora said with an honest-to-goodness cackle.

"Like for nukes? Is that seriously what y'all are looking for? Is this the 1960s?"

"The nuclear launch system is disastrously simplistic, and we only require active codes to start a global war. Mutually assured destruction is a universal concept and—"

I cut the Dora off. "Don't alien-splain to me. We know all that. It just feels super unoriginal. And kind of underwhelming, to be honest."

"It's still a big deal, Chuck," Ghost said.

"I know that, obviously. I was just expecting something more science fiction-y."

"Let the grownups talk," Pax-7 growled.

"Wow, just…wow." I glared at him. "I am *not* going to miss you."

"If I hand the codes over, how do I know you'll send Chuck to us? And we also need your guarantee that both Bailey and Corrin will be safe." Ghost sounded like he had a handle on things. This was reassuring.

"We'll meet you at the designated coordinates. I will let your friends live, and you'll hand over the codes," said the Dora.

I had about a trillion questions, but Axa had told me about a trillion times that I needed to stay quiet while there were negotiations between the Dora and my friends. The Cralzod really preferred to feel like they were in charge.

"We need to play it cool, as the kids say," Axa had explained.

"It's me, isn't it? I'm the kids," I'd said, and I kept my mouth shut, which was really, really hard. I wanted to ask about Axa, who I didn't see on the screen, and Corrin and where the hell Ghost had been and how did he get hold of nuclear launch codes. But apparently all of that was going to have to wait because the "grownups" were talking.

"We'll be there," Ghost said, "and General Dora, Chuck better come back to us unharmed."

The Dora winked. "I wouldn't dream of harming her."

Why did she wink? I did not understand flirting.

I really hoped that this whole hostage exchange wouldn't take much longer. I was tired of being a pawn, and now I had to worry about the Earth getting blown up on top of everything else.

Chapter 26

Turned out, I did get to do a spacewalk, and I was really not sure that I ever wanted to repeat that activity. Why, after my previous experience in space, I thought I would enjoy it, we'll never…Oh. ADHD.

The coordinates the Dora shared were on a moon but like a super tiny moon. Think big asteroid-sized moon. Truly, though, sizes in space might never make sense to me.

We arrived there almost immediately, and they piloted the ship very close to the surface but did not land. We floated down with the help of a few handheld mini rocket boosters. They linked us all together and shot a tether from the airlock to the surface of the asteroid moon. Then we clipped onto it with things that looked like carabiners and pulled ourselves down, the little rockets attached to our suits pushing us along.

Those rockets were also there to push us back to safety in case of a catastrophe, I supposed. *Stop thinking about it, Chuck!*

Listen, it was horrifying, and I definitely almost puked. Luckily, they had given me a shot of something like the space version of Dramamine, so I held it together.

I could see the other ship, but it had landed on the surface. Unlike the massive, sleek one that the Dora had, it was smaller and looked as though it had somehow been off-roading like a Jeep in a commercial.

Our groups made their way toward one another, and thankfully, there was enough gravity on that rock to keep me from worrying I might moon-hop off it. I didn't think I would ever be grateful to be literally tied to these folks, yet there we were.

As my friends approached, I could see they were wearing space suits that didn't match. Unlike the black uniform suits the Dora's crew wore, I could see their faces through the helmets. When we got within view and I saw Pacey and Ghost, my knees went weaker than usual with relief. Seeing Ghost on the screen had been one thing—seeing him in the flesh was quite another, and having Pacey in my sights again filled me with excitement.

I started to run ahead for a hug, but the Dora yanked me back rudely.

When we were within earshot, I could tell Pacey was mad.

"Not so fast," the Dora said. "We have to make sure this deal goes smoothly. Or I'll pull the trigger on your friend's timer. I'm guessing at least one of them is in your ship, and that's well within range."

"Just jumping right to the mean stuff as usual, the Dora?" I yanked my arm out of her grip.

"She looks like an evil Kristen Bell," Pacey said to me.

"That's *literally* what I thought. I fucking missed you, Pacey." I beamed at them.

Once again, I wondered where Axa and Corrin were, but the Dora was totally enamored by the shiny metal suitcase Ghost was holding, so I kept my mouth shut.

"I'm sending over Chuck to retrieve the suitcase," the Dora said. "Then I'll send her back with the receiver for your friends."

"Wait, you want me to *hold* it?" I asked. "What if I accidentally push a button?"

"Oh, calm down. There are like ten steps involved," said the Dora. "The likelihood that you push the wrong button and kill your best friends is minuscule."

"You still underestimate my ability to get into awful situations?" I scowled at her. "Even after all we've been through together."

"Fine, I'll put it in a freaking pouch, okay?"

"That would be really helpful. Thank you."

"I am going to be so glad to be rid of teenagers." The Dora pulled a Velcro pocket off her space suit and placed two remote control looking devices inside of it. "Now, walk over there and get me that suitcase."

I nodded and did as I was told. When I got close to Ghost, he looked like he wanted a hug as much as I did, but I knew the Cralzod had twitchy trigger fingers and they were packing *lots* of heat on this little away mission.

I honestly didn't expect to make it very far. Why would they bother keeping us alive if the whole point was to destroy Earth? I wanted to think maybe they had some faith in the younger generations, but the Dora had spent an entire semester at a public school in America, so not freaking likely.

But I supposed I should do as I was told and at least attempt to keep this exchange from going sideways.

Ghost handed me the suitcase and winked. Which made me smile, which made me giggle, which made the Dora snap, "What?"

"What? I laugh when I'm nervous." I shrugged and walked back the way I'd come, which was not the direction I wanted to walk. She narrowed her eyes at me, but I went over and handed her the metal case.

She handed it to one of the others, who scanned it with some sort of handheld device and nodded at her through their helmet.

"Good," said the Dora, satisfied. Then she handed me the pouch with the devices in it. "Yes, well, goodbye, Chuck."

"You're really letting me go?"

"I got what I wanted, power to totally annihilate Earth by setting off a bunch of nuclear weapons." She shrugged.

"Umm, thanks?"

"Oh my gosh, Chuck, stop flirting with me," she said in her best *Clueless* impression.

"You wish. See ya, the Dora." I walked toward my friends.

Just then, there was the sound of a ship's engines powering on. At first, I thought it was the one Ghost and Pacey had flown in on, but then the cable we'd used as a tether to get here snapped, causing the ship to whip around, spinning away from the low parking spot it had been in.

"What the hell?" I said.

Just as Ghost yelled, "Run!"

I didn't need to be told twice and started off. Luckily, the lessened gravity made it easy for me to take off and gain momentum.

"You hit the button a little too early, Axa," Ghost said.

"Is Axa stealing the Dora's ship?" I asked as we hauled ass.

"More like scuttling it," Ghost said.

I wasn't one hundred percent sure what that meant, but it sounded great. Now we just had to make it to our ship before they caught up with us.

And the Cralzod were not happy. I felt the sting of several shots and was really grateful the suit I was in was made to protect from bullets or whatever Taser fire they were throwing at us. But it stung like the dickens.

We didn't have far to run though, and we were able to jump into the ship through a lowered ramp entrance. I turned around just as the hydraulics closed up the walkway with a hiss. I could just make out the Dora in the dust kicked up from the shooting, hands on her hips.

I turned back, followed Pacey down a short hallway to the cockpit of the ship, and plopped down in the first available seat.

"Strap in," they said, pointing to the seat belts behind me.

I did as I was told, and within moments, Ghost had fired up the engines.

"We need some cover fire," he said through his headset, and we could hear shots being fired from above onto the surface. Through the window, we could see Axa wasn't aiming for the aliens but just shooting to block their path.

"I suppose you all have a plan?" I asked.

Pacey turned to me, grinning. "Of course. This was all planned out."

"Okay, but now I can't really tell if you're joking or not."

"Well, we planned *most* of it, and as long as Ghost gets this rust bucket out of range of those weapons, we should be good."

"I don't think they shoot very far," I said, double checking my buckles.

"That's good to know." Ghost beep-booped a few buttons, and we were off.

"Are we just leaving them there?" I asked.

"Just long enough to get back to Earth and warn people to change the nuclear codes if they haven't and, you know, give them a heads-up about the impending doom. Which, to be honest, I'm pretty sure they all know about and are just in denial or else have big plans already. Really, Pacey is the one you can talk to about the deep government stuff."

"Are they going to be okay?" I asked.

"Yeah, they'll probably be rescued any minute, so we don't have much time."

"Are you that worried about Dora?" Pacey asked.

"That's 'the Dora' to me, and I mean, no, she's pretty awful."

"But you think she's pretty?"

"Wow, good to know that literally nothing has changed since I disappeared," I mumbled.

"What was that?" they asked.

"Nothing," I said, suddenly exhausted and very overwhelmed. "Any chance I'll get to take a nap sometime soon?"

"Miles to go, my friend," Ghost said as he maneuvered the ship closer to the Dora's. "As soon as we pick up Axa and Corrin, we're getting out of here."

A few moments later, Axa and Corrin burst through the cockpit and took the remaining seats.

"Howdy, stranger," Corrin said, grinning at me and strapping herself in.

"Time to motor." Axa gave me a thumbs up.

Chapter 27

"We're on the fastest course back to Earth," Ghost informed me. "Pacey, you take the helm. Axa, you and I need to discuss some things. Corrin, how about you show Chuck around."

"Don't you need to turn off the fasten seatbelt sign?" I asked as the others unclipped.

"Come on, Chuck." Corrin offered me her hand as I stood from the seat. We didn't let go as she walked me around the ship.

"Now this is the type of an endearing mismatch of a ship a rag-tag group of do-gooder space pirates would have," I said.

"Um, thanks?"

"Excellent call back, brain," I said, nodding and looking around.

"Did you just compliment your brain for remembering a thought you had?"

"Yup."

"You are such a freaking nerd. I missed you."

"I missed you too. But right now, I really need to pee, and if there's *any* way I could get a cup of coffee, I would give those doomsday codes back to the Dora."

"Come with me." Corrin grinned. We went to the small kitchen, and it was downright cozy.

"How did you all end up on this ship?" I asked.

She gestured for me to sit and began making coffee and pulled out some tins of crackers and peanut butter. "When Ghost went through that portal, a lot happened. He accidentally broke up a whole heist situation with Dora's people and had to go on the run. Because it was so completely bonkers, he didn't know who to trust on Earth or throughout the literal galaxy, so he stayed away and sort of planet- and station-hopped until he got the lay of the land."

"Wow, that is a lot." I nibbled on crackers and cheese while the coffee brewed. I could already smell it, and it felt like a scent gifted from the stars themselves.

"Tell me about it. He'll fill you in more later, I'm sure, but long story short, he's working with a group that basically defends Earth. And it comes with perks, like ships."

"Of course Ghost would be an Earth-defending hero captain." I nodded.

I wanted to spend more time with Ghost right now, but it was also nice to just be with Corrin. I couldn't believe Corrin was here in front of me and because of the Dora she might not have even lived long enough for me to have one of those majorly huge gesture moments.

"I'm sorry I dragged you into this," I said, my voice quaking.

"It's not on you, Chuck. You know that, right?"

"No, really though, it's my fault." I tried to hold my tears in. "If me and Ghost hadn't had the ridiculous idea to jump through a freaking alien portal to who knows where, then none of us would be in this place."

"Okay, well yeah, that's true."

"Wow. Just throw me under the bus."

She laughed. But then started to cry just a bit. And I saw she was shaking.

I reached my hand out and placed it on top of hers.

"I've got you now." I squeezed her hand. "We've got this. No more pity party for Chuck. I'm going to help you get out of this death bug thingy."

"It's been a rough couple of days." Corrin looked up at me.

"Tell me about it." I said in an *I actually want to hear about it way*, not just a commiserating way. There was no chance that whatever happened in this universe could have been anything but bananas for her, and I wanted to hear about every second of it.

But it would have to wait because we needed to figure out how to deactivate the device in Corrin and be ready to do the same for Bailey. I pulled out the pouch that held the controllers and set it on the table, not wanting my clumsy thumbs to mess things up.

Turned out I didn't have to worry about pushing the wrong button.

Because when I opened the pouch and we looked inside, it was just half a dozen nutrient bars. And I swore to the gods I could hear the Dora's smug laugh from across the solar system.

"Well, shit."

Corrin and I went to find Axa and Ghost, who were poring over some schematics and a giant pile of wires and computer chips.

"This doesn't surprise me at all," Axa said when we told them what the Dora had done.

"What do we do?" I asked, trying not to despair. "Is there like an alien science bomb squad that can dismantle it?"

"No, but we'll get it sorted out at the next negotiation." Ghost put his hand reassuringly on Corrin's shoulder.

"Why will that one go any better than last time?" I asked.

"Well, for starters, we have her ship." Axa nodded to the jumble of computer bits strewn across the table.

"Huh?" I said intelligently.

"It's basically the ignition and key," Ghost said. "Axa is going to make some adjustments before we give it back."

"Plus, this time, they don't have you." Corrin looked at me, eyes soft. "So we have way less to lose."

"It doesn't seem like that to me." I took a seat and fiddled with some wires.

Axa's hand closed over mine. "Don't touch that, Chuck."

"Why don't you get some rest?" Ghost suggested. "We'll have some food later after Axa and I finish this. One of us will come wake you up."

It felt like I was being dismissed, but when I went to the bathroom and saw the bags under my eyes, I realized Ghost was just looking out.

Corrin led me down a narrow passageway to the crew quarters.

"The ship is pretty small, so it's expected people just sleep in shifts most of the time. So we don't have assigned bunks." Corrin showed me the room that had two sets of bunk beds and a small window looking out at the stars. Each bed had thick quilts and throw pillows, and there were reading lamps hooked at the head of each one.

I sat down and pulled off the boots that were part of my borrowed Cralzod space suit.

"Want me to read to you?" Corrin sat at the edge of the bed as I flopped down.

"Hell yes," I said. And I was asleep before she got through a single page.

A few hours later, Pacey poked their head in and said, "Time to eat."

I groggily sat up. Corrin had fallen asleep with her arm draped across my waist, and I would never forgive Pacey for waking me up. But then my tummy rumbled, and I smelled something greasy.

"Is there more coffee?" I asked as Corrin stirred and sat up too.

"Of course, my friend," Pacey said.

I pulled on my boots and grabbed my cane, following Corrin to the small kitchen area.

Axa was sitting next to Ghost, and they had obviously been talking about something involving me because, as soon as I walked in, they stopped.

"Um, what's up?" I said.

"We were just trying to decide how best to fill you in," Ghost said.

"We know each other," Axa blurted, and it might have been the first time I'd seen her actually squirmy.

"Yeah, I know that. Me, Chuck. You, alien," I said.

"No." Axa gestured between herself and Ghost. "I mean *we*."

"What, you and Ghost?" I asked.

"Yes," Axa said. "We've been working together, and I'm sorry I didn't tell you."

"I kinda figured that out while y'all were rescuing me from the Dora."

"I feel bad that I kept it from you during our captivity."

I held my hand to hers like she'd shown me. "Look, I am *not* good at keeping secrets. Like, for *real* not good at it."

"Yes, I garnered that from the large number of things you told me."

"How long have you all known each other?"

Ghost had been getting coffee for everyone and answered as he stirred his. "Axa was one of the first defenders I met when I followed the vague instructions I'd been given and hopped through the portal. She has been working with some other alien groups to help defend Earth against people like the Cralzod who want to see it destroyed."

"Whoa, so you both go way back."

"Yes," Ghost said. "Axa's team had contacted me, and I began working with them. One of my first assignments was to intercept the Dora's crew, which was attempting to steal the nuclear codes. Then *someone*"—Ghost continued, looking at Pacey, eyebrows raised—"decided they should get all involved." He looked back to me

"It surprised me," Axa said, "when it was you who was thrown into the Phuphrath prison and not Pacey."

"We knew Pacey was in trouble with them," Ghost said, "and the team sent Axa to get captured so that when they inevitably caught up to Pacey, the two of them could escape together."

"We were unaware just how much of an interest the Dora had with you, Chuck," Axa said.

"She's a *total* stalker." Corrin crossed her arms.

"Once Corrin and Pacey went through the portal, they were able to get in contact with me pretty quickly," Ghost continued. "We thought it was going to be a simple rescue from the Phuphrath."

"Was no one else worried about those guys?" I asked, looking at Pacey and Corrin for affirmation.

"Turns out there are way worse things out there," Pacey said somewhat sheepishly.

"Anyway," Ghost went on, "once the Dora got involved, we knew you and Axa were in serious trouble. General Dora is not known for her mercy."

"Go on and say it. She's a douche canoe," I said.

"Based on the context, I will agree," Axa said.

"What you and Axa did was amazing, Chuck." Corrin squeezed my hand. "Such good thinking with Pacey's tracker."

"I still can't believe you put that on me," I said.

"I have a total of zero regrets." Pacey shrugged.

"So, what do we do now?" I asked.

"Now we have some dinner," Ghost said, "and hope we make it to Earth in time to stop the codes from working and that Dora is pissed enough about her ship to free Corrin and Bailey."

Chapter 28

When we re-entered our solar system, I actually got to watch out the window as we approached Earth this time, which was breathtaking, since I wasn't being imprisoned, though I was equally nervous.

We had a deadline, and as Ghost put it to someone on the radio, we were "coming in hot."

What happened next included a lot of *and thens* because, whew. Right.

Turned out that even though Earth itself was way behind on our intergalactic relations and travel and general awareness, that didn't mean other species hadn't taken notice, and the Earthly powers that be needed to step up and fast.

We were pretty sure they at least knew the Cralzod had the codes, and Ghost contacted his people, who relayed the message all the way to the top. So, fingers crossed, the nuke situation was being handled, and the Dora couldn't just press a couple buttons and destroy us all.

Now, our biggest problem was a pissed-off the Dora who was presumably not at all happy with being stranded on an asteroid, having her ship rendered unusable, and with soon to be, if not already, expired nuclear codes. She had obviously expected a double cross, since she too had instigated her own double cross, so I was sure this was going to be a super pleasant gathering.

Our primary concern was disabling those ticking time-bomb death robots inside my best friends.

"For once, I think I should do the talking," I said as we approached Earth.

"What do you mean?" Ghost asked as he instructed us to buckle up.

"I think I can get through to her," I said, and it sounded right, though I was not completely sure why or what I planned to say.

"What makes you think that? She has betrayed you like a *lot* of times." Corrin crossed her arms.

I didn't want to hope too hard that she was maybe a little jealous, but also, I couldn't help but hope she was a little jealous. Because I was an unfocused disaster human.

"Sure, but we also had a lot of time to get to know each other. And I think I can reason with her, at least enough to save you and Bailey," I said, more certain by the minute.

"Okay, but how will she know where to meet us?" Corrin asked.

"It's obviously going to be at the quarry," I said with a shrug.

"I mean, yeah, that makes sense," Ghost agreed. And I was really grateful he was back.

Ghost landed the spaceship—holy shit, we were in a spaceship!—at the quarry. Definitely the quickest way to get there.

"Aren't people going to see this?" I asked.

He cackled. "Ha, people don't notice anything. It is absurd. And also explains a lot of the things we got away with." I didn't want to notice he used "got" instead of "get," but this whole reunion had been not how I imagined.

"Fair enough," I said, and we unbuckled our harnesses and stood up.

I realized I was going to need my cane and also that I had no idea where I'd stuck it. And then Corrin was there holding it out to me, just like she always had before this whole interstellar excursion. Finding it before I ever realized I needed it. I stood up a little taller before I let the warm feelings take over and distract me from what was coming next.

Fortunately, I was dressed like a badass space assassin. So I was ready to do badass space shenanigans. I always said, dress for the planet-saving job you wanted, not the planet-saving job you had.

We walked down the ramp and stood near the quarry's edge.

"I am glad to see this quarry of yours, Chuck." Axa came to stand with us. She held the modified ignition to the Dora's ship. "If it comes up in your negotiation, I'd really appreciate you get my own ship communicator back."

"I got you, pal." I patted her on the shoulder.

There wasn't much time before the Dora arrived, and I took Corrin's hand, giving it a squeeze. We stood with our backs to the ship looking out at the water.

"You know she killed all those blob guys?" I said.

"She did?" Corrin turned to me, shocked.

"Yeah, I mean, they weren't my favorites, but she spaced them," I said, my voice shaking. "I just need you to know. I'm going to do anything I can to keep anything bad from happening to you."

"I know that," she said. "And same. I'd go on a space adventure to rescue you any time."

Just then, the sound of engines broke the momentary stillness, and a ship that looked very similar to the Dora's but was much smaller landed about a hundred feet from ours, kicking up dust and rocks. The Dora and her crew, along with five or six additional Cralzod that I didn't recognize, came out of the smaller ship in what could only be described as a huff.

"You stole my ship," the Dora growled at us.

"We've deactivated your weapons, so there's no need to point those things at us," Pacey shouted across at them. Axa and Pacey had figured out how to put out a relay that disabled the weapons, since the Cralzod tech was all connected through their ships and we had the keys.

It was all very technical, and I did not follow it. But Axa had assured me the Dora couldn't just shoot us now.

The Dora looked down at her blaster and was definitely not happy with what she saw because she groaned and stuck it back in the holster.

"Give. Me. Back. My. Ship," she demanded.

"Give us the right remote for the detonators, and maybe we will," I yelled back.

"And the launch codes?" Ghost asked. We were hopeful they'd been changed, but also, tons of things seemed to be going wrong.

"My ship is worth more than three of your disgusting planets. Keep your codes." She nodded to Pax-7, who threw the suitcase back over to us.

"Wow. That was really harsh, the Dora." I frowned at her. Corrin and Pacey looked at me funny.

Axa cleared her throat.

"Oh yeah," I said, "And give Axa her watch back."

"This deal is getting worse and worse for me," the Dora said through gritted teeth, eyes aflame.

"I thought your ship was worth the most of anything." I crossed my arms. "Or are you saying it's *not* worth the most?"

"I want one more thing." The Dora took a step closer.

"Oh yeah, what's that?" I thrust my chin out in what I was sure was a determined and quite menacing way.

"A kiss."

"What?"

"Oh my god, Chuck, stop flirting with me."

"What is going on?" This was Pacey.

"I was just kidding," she said, smirking maniacally and literally flipping her ponytail around.

"I mean, yeah, I knew that," I said. "Now fix my friends."

The Dora pulled another pouch from her belt.

"How do we know that's the right one?" Corrin asked.

The Dora pulled it out and quickly pressed a series of buttons. Suddenly, Corrin shook, and then she fell to the ground. It looked like she was having a seizure.

"What did you do?" I knelt down beside Corrin, staying close but not touching her.

The Dora waved her hand dismissively. "Always so dramatic."

"Stop hurting her!" I yelled.

Just then, Corrin let out a tiny cough, and a glowing green Tic Tac-sized cylinder fell out of her mouth. She took in a deep, shuddering breath and sat up quickly, backing away from the device.

"She'll be fine," the Dora said. "Now, I'll take my ship back."

"What about Bailey's thingy-ma-bob?" I made a gimme gesture.

The Dora sighed at me, for what I really hoped was the last time, and tossed over a small controller. Which I thankfully didn't have to catch because Axa held out her hand and snagged it for me.

"And my watch?" Axa held out her other hand.

Rolling her eyes, Dora handed it over. Axa looked relieved and slipped the band around her slender wrist.

"Your ship, Dora." Pacey gave the control panel to the Dora, who looked it over with a scowl.

"Leave your Tasers," Ghost added, "All of them."

I helped Corrin to her feet and gave the Dora a little wave. "Really not going to miss you, Dor."

Backing away, the Dora and her crew boarded their ship, and in an excessive amount of dust—I really thought she did it on purpose—they took off and were gone.

Just then, half a dozen IRL Men in Black came out of the woods, guns drawn, but only for a second.

Ghost stepped out in front of us, and they lowered their weapons as he said, "My handle is Ghost, I've been working with Colonel Reynolds. My access code is 56324. And the call is negative."

He paused and waited while one of the suits radioed in to someone, whispering into their collar, and got what I assume was a good response? Because they nodded at Ghost, and just said, "We will be in touch."

And then they scooped up the weapons the Cralzod had left and straight up melted into the forest.

"Um, Ghost," I started, "are you a badass? Is that what is happening?"

He smiled at me and shrugged. "I mean, I might be, at least a bit, of a badass."

I hugged him for real for the first time in ages. And it felt so good. I needed us all together.

Suddenly, there was a loud crash through the forest toward the trail entrance. We all spun to face whatever new horror awaited us.

Of all people, Bailey burst from the tree line.

He clutched his side, panting. "What did I miss?"

Chapter 29

"**G**host! Oh my god." Bailey gaped at Ghost and looked around at the group. "Where the blazes have y'all been?"

"Long story, my friend." I walked over to him. "You're going to need to brace yourself. This is going to hurt, but we gotta do it fast."

"It's not that bad," Corrin said.

"What's not that bad?" he asked just as Axa, wasting zero time, punched in the code to eject the Cralzod device. Similarly to Corrin, after a few shaky moments, it popped out.

"What the hell?" he asked, coughing.

"To summarize," I said, holding out my hand to help him up, "I was one hundred percent correct about basically everything, and you all should defer to me for alien matters going forward."

"Right, so that is *not* what we learned, but Chuck was right about a few things," Pacey conceded.

"A *lot* of things," I corrected them.

"More like right about a few things that happened to be really important?" Corrin said helpfully.

"We should probably get home and talk to your parents. They are freaking out," Bailey said. "Regardless of whether Chuck was right about anything or not."

Axa cleared her throat. "I'm going to stay here until my ship arrives. This portal has been permanently disabled, and I don't know Earth well enough to wander around a small town."

"I can't stay either," Ghost said.

"What?"

"Excuse me?"

"Huh?"

"Like hell."

The four of us spoke at once.

"This is complicated, I know. But the past six months have been really eventful." Ghost was clearly not sure how to say what he needed to say.

"Just say what you need to say," Corrin said, and I freaking loved her.

As a good friend. Calm down.

"I've done more for Earth the past months than I could ever do as Samuel," he said. "You all have known me as Ghost and seen the best in me my whole life, but that's not how it is with most people. I can keep helping. Keep the peace and all that."

"But your family…" Corrin started.

"But what about us?" I said at the same time.

"I'll be back. You just have to trust that." Ghost had the audacity to pat me on the freaking shoulder.

I shrugged him off.

"I knew you were going to come back and that we'd find you, but now you're just leaving?" I asked, my voice shaking. "And you?" I turned to Axa. "I thought we were friends?"

She looked at me and said, "I'm almost out of pet food."

"Wait, what?" I said. "What kind of pet?"

"It's really cute, kind of like one of your Earth geckos, but with tiny horns."

"Well, that sounds incredibly adorable," I said. "But stop distracting me."

"You expect us to just hang out here and what? Finish high school without you?" Corrin asked, hands on her hips. She stepped close to me.

I could feel the warmth coming off her, and I only half cared about Ghost and Axa leaving.

"Look," I said, crossing my arms and scowling at both of them, "I'm not letting you both leave without even *one* night of hanging out with us while we're not in immediate danger."

"I'm with Chuck," Pacey said, also crossing their arms.

"Same," said Corrin. "But can we do it at one of our houses? I really, really need a shower."

"If we do that, we'll have to answer a trillion questions that our parents have," I said.

"I mean, I have my camp shower with me," Bailey interjected excitedly. Corrin gave him a look that cleared up any hope he might have had of getting to demonstrate said shower.

"There are showers on my ship." Axa looked down at her fancy watch. "Which should be here any second. You can meet Gizmo."

"Its name is *Gizmo*?" I squealed.

And like magic, a sleek ship landed next to us where the Dora's ship had been just minutes before.

"You are so cool." I put my hand up at Axa, who took it in her palm.

"Okay, okay, I'll try out this alien ship shower, but does this mean the two of you will stick around for the night?" Corrin looked between them hopefully.

Ghost nodded, and Axa said, "That's fine with me. I suppose if I enjoy Chuck's friends half as much as I enjoy Chuck, it could be quite... enjoyable."

"It's settled then," Corrin said. "You are both staying, and we're going to figure out how an alien shower works."

"You know that when we say we're staying, it's for the night, right?" Ghost said as we walked toward Axa's ship.

"I want to meet your pet, Axa," Pacey said.

When we got to the door to the ship, it slid to the side, and we all stepped in, except for Bailey. We turned and saw him, mouth agape, staring at the ship. Come to think of it, I wasn't really sure when Bailey had stopped talking and just started staring in awe at all of us.

I walked up to him and slung my arm across his shoulders. "Come on buddy, you'll get used to the whole aliens-among-us thing before you know it."

After Ghost, Corrin, and Pacey all took showers, we scrounged for food that wasn't even reminiscent of nutrient bars, and gathered firewood in our usual spot overlooking the quarry. Axa and I had been really taken care of hygiene-wise with the Cralzod, so we didn't really need showers. It tied into their clean and smudge-free aesthetic.

Plus, I was still feeling really cool looking in my black spacesuit. I was guessing the Dora would be in trouble for not getting it back from me because I was pretty sure these things were pricy as heck.

Bailey had fun snooping around the ship, though I didn't think it counted as snooping if Axa gave him permission. But eventually, everyone was outside, and we had a fire going. I considered asking if someone wanted to go pick up the makings for s'mores, but I also wanted to keep the most important people in my entire life in the same place for as long as I could.

I lowered myself down gently and took a seat between Corrin and Ghost . I was definitely sore from all the space battles and imprisonment and such. Maybe I could get my folks to start doing those made-up stretching exercises with me when I got back.

The fire was crackling in earnest, and I looked around at all my people.

"Tonight isn't going to be long enough to really get caught up on everything, is it?" I asked Ghost quietly, leaning my shoulder into his.

"No, I don't think it is." He poked at the fire with a long stick. How he always found one long enough to do that, I'd never know.

"Well then, tell me one most exciting thing, and I'll tell you one most exciting thing," I suggested.

"Let's go around *Thanksgiving say what we're thankful for family dinner* style," Corrin said.

I grinned at her in the flickering firelight.

So, we did just that. Going around and taking turns telling stories about what we had been through the last months or days. Even Axa joined in. When she told us about the literal flotilla of Cralzod ships she'd disabled on her own before letting herself be caught by the Phuphrath, I was even more impressed with her than I had been before.

Everyone got to see her glow when Bailey told us about some run-ins he'd had with venomous snakes in the area while searching for us. Apparently, that really creeped her out.

Fortunately, everyone's exclamations of awe didn't seem to faze her, and I was guessing that was thanks to so many hours of human conditioning she'd had with yours truly. Plus, we'd gotten most of our exclamations out of our system when she'd produced Gizmo and it immediately began hopping between all of us.

At one point, Ghost began to apologize to me for what happened at the portal, but I held up my hand and stopped him. "You didn't know."

"But I should have been there for you afterward," he said, frowning.

"We got through it." I squeezed Corrin's hand and smiled at Bailey and Pacey. I didn't want to spend our one night together reliving the night Ghost disappeared. There were too many adventures to hear about.

"Will you tell us how your date with the Dora went?" I asked Bailey, against my inner voice telling me it might be too fresh in his mind.

"About how getting stood up at a high school formal dance goes for most people, I suppose." He grimaced.

"I'm so sorry we weren't there to back you up," Corrin said, genuinely meaning it.

"Well, I'm not," I said.

"What?" said Corrin. Pacey and Ghost both gaped at me.

"Y'all, I told Bailey and Corrin that the Dora was evil like all the freaking time," I said. "You weren't there. No one *ever* listens to me."

Corrin and Bailey looked at each other sheepishly.

"I mean, she's not wrong," Corrin said. Then she slapped me playfully on the arm. "But you could say it nicer."

"Thank you for admitting it," I said, satisfied. "I'm also really glad neither of you got blown up from the insides."

"Yeah, that part would have sucked," Bailey said. "I just don't understand how Dora never got to you."

"One must keep her frenemies at arm's length at all times." I steepled my fingers sagely.

"Well, the date definitely didn't make me want to repeat being stood up," Bailey said. "I may never date again."

"Cheers to that," Pacey gave a thumbs up.

Ghost went on to tell us some truly unbelievable tales of escapes and near misses. Though if anyone was going to barely skirt past an enemy blockade, it would be him. It didn't sound like he'd gotten much studying in though, and Corrin asked if he was going to finish off senior year.

"I'm going for a more holistic, universal education at this point," he said. And I tried not to think too hard about the fact that he was going to be leaving in the morning.

"Well, we're going to miss you, almost as much as last time," Corrin said, leaning over me to squeeze Ghost's knee.

"Almost?" he asked.

"Well, yeah. Now you have to write to us, and we know you're not actually dead. So this time it won't be nearly as much torture."

"Yeah," he said, "sorry I left you alone with the yahoos."

"Watch it dude," I said, smiling.

"You all truly do bond over this shared ribbing, don't you?" Axa looked at us, bemused.

"Yes. Yes, we do." Pacey grinned at us. "I'll be their yahoo any day."

"I do not know what a yahoo is," Axa said.

Corrin rattled off over half a dozen synonyms. We all gaped at her.

"What? I've been studying for the SATs, like all of y'all should be," she scolded us.

"So, Axa, are you heading home?" Bailey asked.

She shook her head. "After I debrief with my commanders and pick up some food for Gizmo, I will continue helping knowledgeable humans navigate potential alliances with other species in this sector of space."

"And you'll rescue me if I get thrown into an impossible situation again?" I asked.

"Please, do not do that." Axa looked very concerned that I might end up in exactly the sort of situation that would require her to rescue me.

"Only if you promise to visit," I said, "even when things are not horribly dangerous."

"As long are *you* promise not to do anything horribly dangerous on purpose?" she said.

"Deal."

We stayed up for the rest of the night, until the sun rose over the water in subtle purples and pinks, and we all sat side by side, legs dangling over the edge of the quarry.

Axa and Ghost had permanently dismantled the portal, so we didn't have to worry about it being used for nefarious reasons, and they didn't have to worry about me randomly jumping through it because I was bored.

Though it would still be a while longer before I felt ready to jump off anything, portal related or not.

When the sun had peeked fully over the horizon, Ghost and Axa looked at one another and nodded that it was time to go.

They stood. The six of us walked over to the ships somberly.

I wondered if there was a flying equivalent to a driver's test and if Ghost should actually be allowed to pilot a spacecraft because he was historically not a great driver of human cars and it took him more tries to get his license than any of us.

But focus, brain. They were leaving.

"No one is going to believe us," I said.

"Good, like seriously, Chuck, don't talk to people about this, any of it," Ghost said. Then he gave a small nod to Axa, and the two of them walked toward the ships.

Axa stopped and gave me a quick hug. "I'm glad you were imprisoned on several alien ships with me, Chuck. If I didn't have to get food for Gizmo, I might stick around for a while longer."

"Y'all better write or send us a beam or whatnot," Pacey said. "And bet I'm going to find my own other way off this rock."

"I'm counting on it." Ghost held them close, bumping foreheads.

"I'm never not going to be upset about this moment." I held back tears that I wasn't sure were from sadness or anger or relief or all of those.

"Sounds about right," Ghost said, and he climbed onto his ship.

Axa followed close behind and made her way into her own ship. She put her hand up in the flat way that showed solidarity.

And then, within moments, they were both gone.

The four of us were left on the edge of the quarry, dust swirling in their wake.

After a few moments, Bailey turned to us. "Seriously, what the heck did I miss?"

Corrin looped her arm around his shoulders, and we all turned together to start the walk back to town. "So much, my friend, but we will fill you in on the rest."

"Actually, I had a pretty good idea for an RPG campaign we could incorporate this into," Pacey said., which led to a huge grin from Bailey.

"And there's no rush. We'll stick together." I put my arm across Pacey's shoulders.

We slowly made our way back to our suburb and cell phone coverage where we could call our parents.

Chapter 30

Our parents were more relieved than anything, when we finally walked back to town and got hold of them all. All our cell phones were dead, including Bailey's because, even though he hadn't left town, he was still the type of person who forgot to charge his cell phone like eighty percent of the time.

I'd left mine on a Phuphrath ship somewhere in space, which meant I'd probably have to get the dreaded flip phone that my parents were always threatening me with since I broke mine all the time.

My folks were, of course, really freaking out. Bailey had been talking to them every day and let everyone know what was going on as well as he could. Though I wasn't sure if they believed him or not. And if they did, I wasn't sure it made things better.

I was really grateful when, instead of grounding me or asking me a trillion questions, they let me shower and go to sleep in my own bed before we had any big talks. My mom had even changed the sheets so they were fresh, and they didn't comment on my spacesuit, though I'm pretty sure it helped them realize I was being serious when I briefly mentioned aliens and space prison.

And I didn't fight it at all when they sat on my bed and rubbed my back while I fell asleep.

When I woke up the next morning, having slept like a full eighteen hours, Arty was curled up under the comforter with me, his curls in my face and his body laying at a diagonal across the bed, just like I'd never left.

I nudged him, "Hey, scout."

He opened his eyes and blinked at me. "I knew you'd come back, just like you said Ghost would."

"Of course. I wouldn't have a grand adventure out in space and not come back to rub it all in your face. No way." I snuggled him a little closer and gave him a kiss on the head. "Now, scoot. I need coffee like you have no idea."

We both trekked to the bathroom and made foaming faces at each other in the mirror while we brushed our teeth then headed to the kitchen.

It felt even homier than before. The light greens and soft browns of the cabinet, my mom's vintage dishes and kitschy hand towels with puns about paper towels and Brussels sprouts on them, and best of all, someone had already made the coffee.

"Bless you, my child." I gave my mom a pat on her shoulder. She was sitting at the table ignoring the newspaper while I added half and half to my coffee then sat down across from her and leaned my cane against the table edge.

Bailey came over later, and so did Pacey and Corrin. He filled us in on the day-to-day things that had happened while we'd been gone, and Pacey and Corrin told us about the adventure they'd had with Ghost tracking me down. All of us knew that there was too much to tell in one day or night and that we really couldn't rush each other to get all the information out. So, we focused on the highlights and piecing things together.

Turned out the Dora had been chatting up the three of us since the beginning of the summer. If it had been up to Bailey, she would have infiltrated our group much earlier.

"She was the fifth player I wanted to invite to our D&D game," Bailey said sheepishly. "It probably would have sped all of this up if y'all had let me invite her."

"Speaking of your failed date," Corrin said, "did you at least get some photos of yourself all dressed up? Chuck and Pacey missed it."

"Yeah, I have pictures. I just wish she wasn't in them."

"How come?" Pacey asked.

"I mean, she took off thirty minutes into the dance without warning and tried to kill all of my friends. Kinda hoping that's not how another date I have goes ever."

"Dude," I said, patting him on the shoulder, "your bar is so low right now."

"It's still pretty cool that you went to a dance with an alien." Pacey took Bailey's phone and flipped through the photos.

Ghost was the biggest mystery for all of us though, and that ache of him being gone was still there. I wondered what to tell his parents, but then Pacey spoke up.

"He gave me a letter for them. I delivered it last night," they said somberly.

"What did they say?" Corrin held her hand to her face.

"They just thanked me and said they needed to read it alone," Pacey said. "I don't know what was in it, but they called me later and said they were very thankful to me for delivering it to them."

"That's a lot," I said. "I would have gone with you."

"I know," Pacey said. "I didn't mind though. Whatever big thing he's involved in, it's important. But I wish he was going to be around to finish out this year with us."

"I can't believe our parents are making us go back to school tomorrow." Corrin groaned.

They'd all gotten together and decided the best thing for us was to get "back to normal," so we had to go right back to classes tomorrow and meet with our teachers to figure out the best plan to make up the work we'd missed.

"Hey, I've had to be at school by myself for almost two weeks. This is the *least* you can do," Bailey said.

Pacey shrugged. "I mean, I've basically kept up with all my online work, so I'm in decent shape."

"How in the world did you pull that off?" Corrin shrieked and threw a pillow at Pacey.

"Wi-fi?" they said like it was the simplest answer in the world.

"You all amaze me," I said. They all looked at me like I was going to say something else. "No, just…that's all. You're amazing."

Corrin furrowed her eyebrows at me.

"What? I'm not being sarcastic." I laughed.

"What is this, Chuck?" Corrin asked me three weeks later when we met up. She was wearing a black sequin jumpsuit and purple heels. Her hair was in coils speckled with gold and wrapped into an elaborate crown atop her head. And yes, I did just use the term 'atop' like I am a scribe describing an ancient goddess statue.

"I don't know if you can use this." I handed her a flower crown that matched the one I was wearing. Peonies and rosemary and those tiny, white bell flowers. I wasn't sure what they were called, but I knew she really liked the way they smelled.

"I can make it work." She turned toward the mirror in her entry hall. Using both hands, she placed it on her head and looked even more like a queen than she usually does.

"Be back by midnight," her mom said and gave me a wink.

"I'll have her back, ma'am," I said, straightening up.

"Sure, just be safe, you two."

"We will, Mom. Love you," Corrin said, giving her mom a peck on the cheek, and we went out to her car together.

"Safer than usual," her mom added as she waved to us from the front porch.

"So, are you going to tell me where we're going?" Corrin asked.

"Where do we always end up?" I rolled my eyes at her for once.

"The quarry? Are you kidding me?" She sighed and visibly stiffened.

"Just trust me," I said, and she looked at me side eyed. "Okay, not the quarry since we like cannot get across anymore unless we want to totally ruin our outfits and, you know, all the trauma. Head to the zoo."

"The zoo?"

"I'm serious this time."

We drove down the winding road and listened to the Decemberists with the windows down but not all the way down because we didn't want to ruin our flower crowns.

The roads were empty and calm, and the smell of winter was just around the next curve. We got to the park that held the zoo, and I had her go past it to one of those gazebos you can rent out for kid's birthday parties or family reunions.

When we got there, Pacey and Bailey were both dressed up as well. Pacey was rocking a suit top and flowing black skirt, Bailey in the navy blue suit he'd gotten for the dance and I'd convinced him wasn't bad luck.

Earlier in the day, we'd strung up about a trillion twinkly lights, and I had instructed Pacey and Bailey to guard and not touch the charcuterie board before Corrin saw it or our friendship would be over.

"What's going on, Chuck?" Corrin smiled at me as she put the car into park and turned off the headlights.

"I made you a dance, since we missed the last one." I felt even cheesier than I knew I sounded, but we'd been through so much. I could take a little embarrassment.

"It's beautiful." She stepped out of the car.

We walked toward our friends, the food, and the photo booth I'd made with a nebula backdrop and like forty ridiculous props.

"I hope you like all the—" I started.

But she cut me off when she tugged on my hand and turned toward me.

Then, before I could overthink it, we kissed.

It was quick, firm, and tender. We pulled back, and each looked at the other. Then she leaned in again, and we were kissing more fervently than before. After a few moments, we pulled apart, breathing hard and both grinning like elegant goofballs.

"Did you say there is cheese and crackers?" she asked, pulling me along with her to the pavilion.

"Yes, like seven types of cheese." I grinned and squeezed her hand.

"My favorite kind of cheese is seven types." She looked at me, her eyes sparkling in the glittery lights.

"You know, I knew that," I said as we walked up to Pacey and Bailey.

"Let's kick off tonight with a toast." Pacey handed champagne flutes to all of us.

"Um…" Corrin started to say.

Pacey stopped her. "Yours is sparkling grape juice, since you still have to drive."

We'd managed one mini bottle of champagne to split between us, thanks to Bailey's older sister, who insisted that would be plenty for a toast.

"So, to what are we toasting?" Corrin asked.

"To a banger of a senior year?" Pacey suggested.

"I was thinking more to a way more chill rest of senior year," Corrin added.

"Things will never be the same after this year, will they?" Bailey said.

"No, Bailey, no, they will not. Let's just toast to tomorrow?" I suggested.

"To tomorrow," Corrin said, raising her glass.

"To today," I said.

"To yesterday," Bailey said.

"To the nerdiest people on the planet," Pacey said.

And we clinked our glasses.

"Let's get this party started!" Bailey cranked up the Bluetooth speakers. Together, we took turns playing the best dance songs we could think of and taking about eight trillion selfies on the backdrop.

The only thing missing was Ghost. And now Axa.

But they were where they were supposed to be, I guessed. And maybe the future had some overlapping adventures left for the six of us.

Later that night, after our four-person dance party and way too much cheese, I stepped out of the pavilion and, when I glanced up, saw a shooting star. Moments later, I felt Corrin come stand beside me and loop her arm in mine. Tonight would be a good night.

Acknowledgments

I would be remiss if I failed to note the plethora of people who I never could have done this without. I am so lucky to have more supportive people than I can count in my life, and I wish I could name every single one, but I'll at least hit a few.

Whitney Hill, my writing coach and inspiration and the person who keeps me moving forward to hit my goals. Thank you for your outstanding work and being such an example of what it means to be a driven author.

To my fellow Weirdos who deserve all the rep and all the joy and all the weird books and all the humor in the world. Y'all are my people and I can't imagine life without you. Bri, Courtney, and Kye the community you have built is astounding. Perhaps some day I'll write something that's more than just mild cheddar on the spice meter.

Jeni Chappelle for unknowingly setting up my entire publishing goals deadline during our first conference call. Thank you for using your powers of suggestion for good. And for giving my book a polish that I didn't know it could have.

Writer Greg and the rest of team Lapin and my Twitch writing friends who have been there for me since draft one and all the editing in between. Hail Hydrate!

Huge shoutout to my cousin Ezra who did the incredible cover art and whose illustrations kept me motivated when I was bogged down with the nuances of publishing.

To Andy, my bookstagram parent. You have no idea how much your friendship has meant to me. I had no idea what sort of growth I was capable of until you came around. Thank you for raising me.

To Meredith, for being my person.

To Marshall and Gaius. Thank you for putting up with me locking myself in the bathroom to let these worlds out of my head. Hopefully the extra screen time won't cause too much trouble in the long run. I appreciate your support more than I can say.

To my family, for being funny and loving and encouraging and creative and kind. Thank you for all the extra hours of kid watching so I could slip away to coffee shops and library parking lots.I am unbelievably lucky.

To the Foxfire friends for never being surprised when I'm off on another new thing. And to our collective creative writing kiddos. You all inspire me beyond belief. Em, thank you for taking my sloppy words and seeing the good in them.

And to the rag-tag group of friends I had growing up. Y'all are going to see yourselves in this story and you'll know who you are. Like it says on the copyright page, while a work of fiction, this book is full of anecdotes and shenanigans from my youth, and Chuck and her friends love each other like my friends loved each other. I was fiercely accepted and learned to be myself. I'm really glad none of us got too blown up. Surround yourself with nerds who write fanfic and play with foam swords and go to alien conventions with you.

About the Author

Jes lives in Tulsa, Oklahoma with her partner and their kiddo. As well as two weenie dogs, Rocket Xavier and Fable Rose Pond. Jes is a Science-Fiction & Fantasy YA author whose works are full of ensemble disaster queer casts and the occasional crime and/or alien. She loves board games, soft sci-fi shows, and using stickers in her planner.

"Chronicles of My Alien Invasion Life" is her debut novel.

For updates about her current and upcoming words, visit: *JesMcCutchenWrites.com* by scanning the QR code below.

CPSIA information can be obtained
at www.ICGtesting.com
Printed in the USA
LVHW110022221222
735706LV00004B/277